TRIPLINES

Leonard Chang

Black Heron Press
Post Office Box 13396
Mill Creek, Washington 98082
www.blackheronpress.com

ISBN 978-1-936364-09-1

Black Heron Press
Post Office Box 13396
Mill Creek, Washington 98082
www.blackheronpress.com

For Toni Ann

PART I

A Normal Saturday Night

1

The night begins with Lenny's father, Yul, sitting in his lounge chair, a tall glass of whiskey on the armrest. He listens to the large stereo under the TV, the turntable encased in an ornate oak cabinet that required three muscular and sweaty men to carry into the house. The Chang family moved here from New York City, from a small dingy apartment on 110th—in between Central Park and East Harlem—to Merrick, Long Island, a commuter town with a railroad station high up on a concrete platform. Yul wanted a house—he had talked on many occasions about his dream to have his own yard, and the privacy they had never had in the various apartments they'd lived in. So he took out a huge mortgage, one that would oppress him for years, especially as his jobs became precarious.

Yul sips Jack Daniel's first from his tall glass, the caramel brown color reminding Lenny of furniture polish, but eventually he drinks straight from the bottle. The strong alcohol smell wafts through the house. The record on the stereo is Prokofiev, *Peter and the Wolf*, which he bought for his children but ends up listening to himself.

Lenny tries to stay in his bedroom, pacing, occasionally doing push-ups or sit-ups, stretching on the cool wooden floor. It's too late to go out, too early to go to sleep. He knows his father is getting drunk, and can hear the low mumblings that mark the beginning of a bad night. Yul talks to himself when he drinks, and although Lenny can't understand Korean, he can easily interpret the rumblings of an unhappy man.

He checks on his younger sister, Mira, who is seven. She's small and frail with chubby cheeks. She has a page-boy haircut with sharp bangs, and hugs herself when she's scared, as she is this particular night. She sits cross-legged in her room with her books and looks up at Lenny with wide, uncertain eyes. She blinks, waiting for him to say something. She tilts her head toward the living room, listening to their father bark something angrily.

Lenny says, "You stink." He shuts the door and hears her sigh.

He returns to his bedroom and plays with his knife collection. Mostly penknives, a few lock blades, and a couple of Swiss Army knives, the collection is part of his secret stash of weapons. He also has Chinese throwing stars; three homemade nunchucks with various chain lengths; a pair of homemade tonfas, small L-shaped clubs; brass knuckles; and a half dozen staffs in his closet. He bought the Chinese throwing stars and brass knuckles through mail order, a recent discovery. Although at eleven years old he's too young to have a checking account, he learned how to buy a money order from the Post Office, and began receiving martial arts catalogs from around the world. He earns money by raking leaves and shoveling snow.

He wants throwing knives. He wants switchblade knives. He wants sais, thin Chinese daggers, and, of course, ninja swords. These he will have to save up for. He also orders tae kwon do and kung-fu instruction books. He practices by himself in the backyard every day. He even made a punching bag out of a rice sack and old rags, and it hangs off a beam in the boiler room.

He hears his father mumbling louder. Then he hears him bellowing, "What are you looking at?" At first Lenny supposes this is his usual ramblings, but then he hears Mira say in a quiet, frightened voice, "I wanted to get some water."

"Then get it."

Lenny hurries out, walking quickly past the living room, glancing at his father, who stands by the window and stares out onto the darkened front lawn. His broad back is hunched, his left hand holding the bottle loosely in his fingers, his right fist resting on the window frame. The music scratches out of the speakers, crackles layered over symphonic strings, and Yul sways to the rhythm.

In the kitchen Mira stands by the open refrigerator, gripping the pale yellow door with grease stains along the handle. The smell of kimchi eases out, because their mother ferments the cabbage in large jars in the back of the fridge. White packs of tofu in water jiggle as Mira reaches up for a bottle of soda. They hear their father speak sharply in Korean. Mira pauses. She doesn't want to return through the living room, but it's the only way back to the bedrooms. She remains frozen, her arm still extending up to the top shelf.

"Do you want water or not?" Lenny asks.

She shakes her head quickly.

"Soda?"

She shakes her head again.

"Then what are you doing here?"

"I'm not thirsty anymore."

"You're wasting the cold air."

Their father calls to them, telling them to come to the living room. They look at each other.

"Come here now!" he yells.

Lenny and Mira walk out to the living room, where their father totters drunkenly by the sofa. His eyes are half-closed, his arms floating in front of him. He says, "I don't like secret talking. You hide in the kitchen and secret talk. What are you talking about?"

Lenny replies, "What to drink."

"Where is your mother?"

"Church."

"Always secret talk. I am tired of it. Talk talk talk. Every-one lies to me! Why do you all lie?"

Mira steps back and looks at Lenny, frightened.

Their father picks up the whiskey bottle from the table and hurls it toward the fireplace, the bottle spiraling across the living room, and it clanks sharply against the brick, bounces off and slides and spins across the carpet. He laughs, and begins dancing to the music, shifting back and forth on his feet, his hands extended in front of him like a marionette's. A sheen of sweat covers his mottled red forehead. He sings in a hoarse, monotone voice, "Secret talk! Secret talk! Everybody lies to me and gives secret talk!"

Mira bursts into tears. Their father stops dancing. He glares at her and says "What's wrong? Why are you crying?"

She shakes her head, unable to speak.

Lenny says, "You're scaring her!"

"You b-be quiet!" he yells, which only makes Mira cry more.

"Go to your rooms!"

"What did *we* do?" Lenny asks.

Their father rears up, and Lenny knows better than to argue. He grabs his sister's thin arm and pulls her down the hall. She sniffles and wipes her nose.

Lenny says, "Stop that."

"I can't."

He leads her to her room and tells her to read. She nods her head. They hear their father rambling to himself again, and Lenny closes her door softly.

2

His mother isn't at church, but at *sok-keh*, or bible study. Lenny usually clumps his mother's religious activities around this time into one gibbering, incomprehensible mess. That she latches onto Christianity is understandable, given her unhappy and miserable marriage. She goes to church on Sundays and prayer meetings once or twice a week, and Lenny once accidentally stumbles upon one at their house. He hears them before seeing anything—the mumbling prayers in Korean slowly rising in intensity as he walks through the back door and wonders what's going on. The voices are all women, all in Korean, and have a chanting sing-song quality that makes his neck tingle with unease. He creeps toward the living room and peers around the corner. His mother and five other women sit in a circle, bibles on their laps, their heads bowed and bobbing. Their eyes are closed and they mumble their prayers aloud, a few voices cracking with emotion.

Lenny stares at his mother, who seems to be pleading to God. He never knows precisely what she says, but he has a good idea of where her anguish lies.

She's in her mid-thirties, pale and gaunt, and has a Jackie-O hairdo that's sprayed stiff, a style she won't change for decades. She's small, thin and energetic, and she practices yoga long before yoga is popular. Lenny often sees her doing Downward Dog on the carpet, reminding him of a stretching cat. She also does strange eye, tongue, and breathing exercises that are supposed to strengthen her *chi*.

Lenny's memories begin in Merrick, Long Island. When he thinks about his childhood he thinks of Merrick. They live in a large, three bedroom house on William Place, across the street from a Presbyterian church, a block away from the Long Island Railroad station.

The railroad station is particularly memorable. Lenny stands on the station platform, looking out over his town, and he flattens pennies and nickels on the railroad tracks. The warped coins remind him of copper moths.

The train tracks sit on huge concrete structures, smooth and grey and bright in the afternoon sun. Often, after school, when Lenny avoids the bus and walks the three miles along Sunrise Highway, he'll climb up the concrete steps to the top of the station and take in the view.

Although his house is one block away from the station, the church obstructs his view of his street. However, he can see his favorite climbing tree, a maple with a U-shaped branch near the top that fits his back perfectly—so perfectly that he often falls asleep in the branch, awakening with a jerk to find himself twenty feet off the ground.

To the south: his house, more neighborhoods shrouded under leafy trees and utility poles with webbed telephone and electrical wires crisscrossing the streets. To the north: mini-malls, auto shops and small warehouses.

Up here on the platform blue, rippled, plastic wind guards separate the east- and westbound benches. Posters of movies and Broadway shows rattle in the wind. Beyond the blue dividers is a small indoor waiting room with Plexiglas windows scratched and spray-painted with graffiti. Payphones stand at each main column. A few people linger

up here, waiting for the next train, but it's usually quiet before rush hour.

The afternoons are a perfect time to explore the platform,
and Lenny discovers the joy of flattening pennies. He has
to jump down onto the tracks, which always unnerves him
because it's a five-foot drop, and he often has trouble shim-
mying his way back up to the platform. Once, when he first
started doing this, he saw the train lights in the distance and
almost panicked, his hands sweating and slipping off the
edge.

The pennies are flattened and scraped shiny, sometimes
even twisted into artful shapes. They glint in the sun. He
once threw a handful into the air and watched them twinkle
down to the street below.

During one of these penny-flattening sessions he tries to
use the coins in the payphone, tricking it to give him cheap
calls. But the uneven edges cause the flat penny to jam in the
slot. He dials the operator and tells her that his coin is stuck,
and she offers to credit his home telephone number for the
loss of the coin. He doesn't want to give her his real number,
but he says that all he wants to do is make a call.

"You can make a collect call. What's the number?"

Lenny isn't sure what number to give, so offers his home
number but changes the last few digits. When the operator
connects to the line, she asks him what his name is.

"William," he says, trying to deepen his voice, thinking
of his street name.

The man on the other line says, "William? William who?"

Lenny hangs up. He stands there for a while, wondering
whom else he can call collect, impressed by this discovery
of free calls. But he can't think of anyone. He has no friends.

Lenny is being punished for losing Yul's slide ruler—Lenny had used it as a toy and misplaced it—and his punishment had initially been to run around the backyard one hundred times. Minor infractions resulted in this common penalty, but when Lenny begins walking and even resting against a tree and Yul sees him, Yul has already started his nightly ritual with Jack Daniel's.

Yul opens the back door and stands on the steps, staring. He is a barrel-chested blunt man with once muscular arms that have become flabby with age. When he's drunk his face flushes and his usual solid stance wavers, as it does now, and he yells at Lenny to continue running.

Lenny does.

Watching his son with disgust and disappointment, Yul says, "Look how slow you are! Feet up! B-Body straight!" He has a severe stutter that recedes when he's drunk.

Lenny sweats, his thighs burning, but he runs faster. Yul continues to taunt Lenny, who glances up at the kitchen window, where his mother watches from the sink. Her expression is shrouded by the shadows from the young maple tree by the window, but he can sense her familiar concern.

Finally, too exhausted, and long having lost count, Lenny slows down. Yul barks at him to continue, but he can't. He begins walking, and this only sets Yul off more. He hurries down the steps toward Lenny, and Umee rushes to the back door. Yul grabs Lenny's neck and shoves him forward, ordering him to run, but Lenny tells him he can't. He's too tired.

Yul mutters in Korean, and then says in English, "You've been babied too much and are too weak." He points to Lenny's skinny, pale arms. "Can you even do a pull-up? A simple pull-up?" Yul frowns. "Do a pull-up right now." He motions to the swing set that a neighbor had given him years ago; the lime green paint has been overtaken by rust, the swings broken, and neither Lenny nor Mira ever play near this.

Yul pushes him toward the swing set and again orders him to do a pull-up. Lenny reaches for the side bar that's chest high, and he hangs down on it, his feet dragging. But his father tells him to use the top bar.

"How?" Lenny asks.

"Climb up it."

Lenny tries, but flakes of rust dig into his hand, and he whines, "It hurts."

"You must be tougher. This world is too hard on the weak. Get on the b-b-bar!"

When Yul sees his son struggling, he lifts Lenny up easily. Lenny grabs the top of the swing set, but as soon as his father releases him Lenny feels the rust digging into his hands and he lets go.

He falls to the ground, hard, and cries out. He then lies still, breathing in the cool, dewy grass scent.

Umee yells at her husband in Korean. He turns to her and stares without speaking. Umee freezes, and after a moment of his full attention, she looks away. Yul then hoists Lenny back up and orders him to hold on. The rust flakes cut into Lenny's palm and he whimpers. Yul stands behind Lenny and says, "Do not let go. You must be strong."

Lenny's grip loosens, but Yul moves closer behind him and presses a finger into his back, saying, "Don't."

Lenny's vision blurs, his hands stinging, and he feels his shoulders aching. The jabbing finger hurts his back. Lenny lets go of one hand, and Yul says, "Stay on!"

Lenny latches his hands back on, tightly, and feels more cuts in his fingers and palms, and cries out, "It hurts!"

"Stay on!"

But then Lenny falls to the ground, collapsing into a ball, and he cradles his stinging, aching hands. His father nudges his back with his slipper, the toe digging into Lenny's shoulder blade, and Yul says something in Korean, his tone laced with disgust. Lenny's mother runs to him, yelling at his father, who turns and lumbers away.

"Come, Lenny," his mother says quietly, helping him up.

"My hands," he says, shocked by the little beads of blood. "My hands."

"Come inside."

Lenny stares at the blood, at the tiny specks of rust in his palm, and then, finally, begins to cry.

His mother hushes him, telling him it will be fine. She spends thirty minutes plucking out the rust splinters with tweezers, his sobbing muted only by his fascination with the way his blood stains the blotted paper towel, turning it pink. His mother, feigning a smile, tells him his favorite folktale about a bear and a tiger to distract him, but he stares at the blood, mesmerized.

Umee's experiences upon arriving in the U.S. were traumatic. She came to Boston alone for graduate school, knowing no one. She was supposed to stay with a host family, one set up by the school, but the first night she stayed there the husband crept into her room and tried to rape her. She screamed and scared him away, and immediately left the house. She had nowhere to go. She tried the local YWCA, which was fully booked, and it appeared as if she was going to be homeless until she broke down and begged the YWCA administrator for anything, even a sofa. Finally, they found her a bed, and the next day she had to beg another administrator, this one at the Northeastern University Housing and Residential Life offices, to help her find somewhere new to live.

She was terrified of this country, of starting over here after fleeing her discontented life in Seoul, which included an annulled marriage, the circumstances of which were mildly scandalous: the groom's physical and sexual handicaps had not been revealed to her until after the arranged marriage. She tells this and many other stories about herself to Lenny when he's a child; he suffers from severe hay fever and is often unable to sleep. She sits on his bed and talks about everything. He becomes her confidant, even as a child too young to understand everything.

But these were the conditions his mother suffered under

when she arrived here, and she cried herself to sleep every night for two weeks. And it isn't too hard to understand why, when she began receiving letters from Yul, a man she'd never met but whose mother knew her mother—it isn't too difficult to see why Umee found comfort with a Korean man also studying in the U.S., a man who had also been married. He had a baby son whom he had shipped off to Korea. His ex-wife abandoned both him and her baby boy, and Yul was lonely and depressed.

His letters to her were affectionate, even loving. He had learned about her from his mother, and both mothers were conspiring to bring them together. He wanted to meet her. He wanted to be married again. He would take care of her, he promised. They would be a happy family.

Rumors about Yul's marriage worked its way to Umee, as a woman abandoning a newborn baby was gossip that moved swiftly through the small ex-pat Korean community. Umee had even known about the ex-wife when she was a student in Korea—they had gone to the same high school, just two grades apart.

However, Umee didn't know the extent of the violence, the abuse, the drinking.

All she knew was that she was alone in a frightening foreign country, and the soothing words of the man in New York gave her hope.

Both of Lenny's parents work fulltime, his father a computer programmer and his mother a small-business owner. Lenny's mother runs a candy store. You would think a kid with a mother who owns a candy store would be something wonderful, but really, the strongest memory Lenny has about the store is her getting robbed.

It happens around the same time Lenny learns about free collect calls. In fact, he probably learns about the robbery after coming home from the train station with more flattened coins. He wants to make something out of them, possibly a necklace for his mother. He adds the new coins to his jam jar and then prepares for his martial arts training. He has an old tae kwon do manual that's written in Korean, but the photos and drawings are all he needs. He also has Kung-fu books, and tries to combine the kicks of tae kwon do with the hand and fist styles of Kung-fu. He brings his books out into the back yard and starts his stretches. He practices the forms—prescribed sequences of punches and kicks that he memorized from the books—and then works on the various kicks and hand strikes.

They have two large trees in the back yard—a tall oak and a young maple—and he uses the young maple trunk as a target, attacking it with various kicking and punching combinations, though being careful not to cut his knuckles. He tries to emulate some of the sound effects from the

Saturday afternoon kung-fu movies on channel 5. He loves these poorly dubbed Shaw Brothers imports so much that he records them on an audio cassette and listens to them when he goes to bed, imagining the scenes that correspond with the dialogue. The sound effects, with the thwacks and crashes amidst the yelling and grunting, help him envision the movie again.

After Lenny hits the tree until his knuckles and feet hurt, he does push-ups, jumping jacks, and sit-ups. By the time he walks into the house he finds his father sitting in his lounge chair with the TV news on. Yul still has on his dress slacks and button-down shirt, the collar open and the sleeves rolled up.

"Where is your mother?" he asks Lenny.

Lenny says he doesn't know.

"Is she at the store?"

"I don't know."

"What do you know?"

Lenny pauses. "She's usually home by now."

His father grunts and pulls himself up, walking to the kitchen telephone. Lenny hears the rotary dial clicking, and after a moment his father speaks in Korean. The conversation is brief, and he hangs up quickly. He rushes to the closet to get his coat and tells Lenny to watch his sister.

"What happened?"

"Where is your brother?" Yul asks.

"I don't know."

"We will be back later."

"Where's Mom?"

"The store was robbed. Make your sister dinner. We will be late."

He leaves through the front door, which is surprising. They always use the back door, and as Lenny wonders about this anomaly, the news settles in. Robbed.

Sweets 'N Gifts, the small candy store, is in Bellmore, the next town over. This was Yul's idea, setting up a business for his wife to run now that all the kids go to school. Both believe in the American dream of owning their own business, and Yul was especially eager for his wife to start a store that would make them self-sufficient. Instead of a grocery or liquor store, the usual Korean immigrant start-ups, they decided on a candy and small gift store that dealt not in the prepackaged, mass-produced candy the supermarkets sold, but in the old-fashioned loose variety that Umee sold out of large jars with shiny tin covers, weighing and bagging whatever the customer pointed to: rock candies, licorice sticks, lemon drops, and Swedish fish.

The store is in a small commercial strip mall next to a large hardware warehouse, and never has customers. They are losing a lot of money, and it's making their already embattled marriage worse, since Umee blames Yul for the bad idea, and Yul blames Umee for the poor execution.

When Ed comes home for dinner and finds that their parents aren't here he tells Lenny that he's going back out.

Lenny says, "Mom was robbed."

Ed stops. "Is she okay?" He's getting even more muscular, his biceps and chest stretching his old, thin T-shirt. His head looks oddly small. He once told Lenny that he started lifting weights a few years ago to be able to take on their father.

"I don't know," Lenny replies.

"I'll be back later." Ed then disappears through the garage. Lenny has only had glimpses of his brother like this for the past couple of years, and he once heard Ed tell his friends that he was going to get as far away from this house as he could after high school. Their father has always been hard on him, and when they all sat together for dinner he lectured and berated Ed for not being a better student.

Mira appears in the living room as soon as Ed leaves and asks what's happening. When Lenny tells her she asks, "Was Mom killed?"

"No! Are you crazy?" But then Lenny isn't so sure.

"I wrote a book. Look." She shows him a book titled *Me* that she had typed and stapled in between cardboard covers. An "About the Author" section is on the back, with her photo. Lenny is impressed, but also distracted. He tells her, "If Mom is dead, you're going to an orphanage."

She blinks, taking this in.

"*Back* to the orphanage," he adds. "You know you were adopted, right?"

"What?"

As soon as he sees that she considers this a possibility, he spins a story about how their mother couldn't have another baby, so they all went to the orphanage to choose a new one. "You were still a baby, crying and everything. We picked you because you look sort of like me and Mom. Maybe you should write a book about that."

Mira takes her book and wanders back to her room, considering this. Lenny thinks of more ways to torment her, but then wonders if their mother really is dead.

When their parents return home a few hours later, his mother is pale and shaky. Her usually neat hair is disheveled, tufts sticking out. She sits unsteadily at the kitchen table while his father pours them both a drink—whiskey on ice—and she remains subdued. Yul explains that someone came in at closing with a gun and took all the money. The police were there for a while, taking the report.

None of this feels real until Lenny's mother cries for a moment, just a quick sniffle, her face crumpling, and then she shakes this off and sips her drink, the ice clinking. Their father is already on his second glass, this one with no ice, and says something to her in Korean, which makes her face flush. She retorts something harsh, and he stares at her coldly, then mutters something. He takes his glass and the bottle to the living room.

She looks at Lenny and says, "I'm okay."

"What happened?"

She waits a moment, then tells him that a young man, possibly a teenager, with large sunglasses, came in, pulled out a gun and ordered her to give him all her cash. She had eighty dollars in the register. He then told her to get into the back closet, and he shoved a chair under the door handle. She waited a few minutes then broke out and called the police.

"That's all?" Lenny asks.

"He could've shot me," she says.

"Oh."

"We will install a special alarm tomorrow."

"What kind of gun was it?"

She sighs. "I don't know. Go to bed, Lenny."

He returns to his room, passing his father, who stares

angrily at the TV news. The smoldering expression on his face means that he's not finished with his wife, and Lenny prepares for a fight.

It begins with low, sharp murmurs in Korean, their voices modulated because they are aware of their children in the house, but as the fight escalates, with the see-sawing dynamic of Yul retreating to the living room and Umee following him and arguing, and then Umee running into the kitchen with Yul following, they soon forget about the kids and yell at each other in their loudest voices.

Lenny isn't sure what they're saying. Their parents never taught him Korean, and because of speech problems from his cleft palate, a speech pathologist recommended that they speak only English to him. Korean, then, became the language of fighting.

The argument goes on for another forty minutes, and it sounds as if Yul blames Umee for not trying to fight to keep the money. Lenny hears English words sprinkled in, and infers meanings from their tones. Umee accuses him of wanting her dead. The fight quiets down, and then kicks up again a couple of hours later as Yul becomes more drunk. They shift from arguing about money to venting and cursing. Lenny recognizes the Korean curses, the "shangs" and the "michin nyuns" spat at each other. Then he hears his father hitting his mother – a slap, a cry of pain, more yelling, and crying.

His father chases his mother through the house, their steps heavy, his mother wheezing in fear. The floor and walls shake with their steps, and his mother's lighter, quicker footsteps run down the hall and toward his room. She leaps in and locks the door. His father crashes into the door, bellowing in Korean, and bangs his fists for a minute, but, exhausted, he eventually retreats to the living room. They hear glass clinking, the TV going off, and the stereo turning on.

Lenny sits up in his bed. His mother stands in the middle of the room, her fists pressed against her stomach. He smells the familiar mixture of her sweat and his father's alcohol. She sees him in the darkness and tells him to go back to sleep, but his heart beats quickly and he remembers how once his father had once almost crashed through the door. His mother tells him again to go to sleep. He lies down, and reaches under his pillow, holding onto his favorite pair of nunchucks. He made these from an old broomstick, fish-eye screws and a chain from the hardware store. The feeling of them in his hands is reassuring, and he hears his mother lower herself to the floor, waiting until his father passes out. After a few minutes his heartbeat slows and he relaxes into his pillow. He hears his mother sighing.

Lenny falls asleep with the sounds of classical music floating in from the living room.

Lenny has Speech Therapy every Thursday afternoon. He
and three other kids from different grades show up at a
small office near the Janitor's room where they sit at a tiny
table with a young speech therapist, Ms. Feinberg, whose
perky and enthusiastic demeanor helps yank them out of
their post-lunch torpor. She has shelves of toys and devices,
including a blue bubble head-piece that funnels their voices
directly to their ears, so that they can hear their voices acute-
ly, but Lenny doesn't like what he hears. He has a nasal,
high-pitched voice that embarrasses him, and Ms. Feinberg
tries to teach him to block off the airflow to his nose when he
speaks. It's difficult. The cleft palate he was been born with
had been minor—only the soft palate had been split—but it
had been enough to render that muscle useless, so he has a
lot of "leakage." Hard consonants come out soft. Sometimes
he sounds better when he has a cold and his nose is stuffed
up.

The other kids have different problems, lisps and stutters, but they are all similarly frustrated with the exercises
and lessons. They are also similarly embarrassed by their
disabilities, and they rarely talk to each other. They certainly
don't acknowledge each other outside of this room. Once,
when Ms. Feinberg was late, they stood outside the door
silently, not even looking at each other.

This session Ms. Feinberg rips up small pieces of tissue,
places them on a piece of cardboard, and holds this up to

Lenny's nose. She tells him to say, "Sally sells seashells by the seashore." He does this, and the air from his nose moves the tissue pieces. Ms. Feinberg instructs him to practice this now without moving the tissues. "Don't let air out through your nose."

Lenny tries, but the leakage keeps fluttering the tissue pieces. She gives the others different tasks. One of the kids, the stutterer, has to recite the same line but with a wooden tongue depressor in his mouth. He stutters over the line and almost gags. The two lispers also repeat the line, but with the bubble head-piece on, the light blue plastic making them look like astronauts. All of them now recite the line, out of sync, in monotones, and it has the chanting quality of Lenny's mother's bible study group.

After school Lenny waits patiently for Mira, because he promised he'd walk home with her. She appears at the entrance with an armload of books, her blue sweater buttoned crookedly, and he tells her that it's a long way with all those books. "You should take the bus."

"But it left already!"

Lenny loads half of the books into his back pack, and starts walking. She hurries after him, asking him to wait up.

Lenny has already explored the neighborhoods during his roaming lunch periods, when he'd eat the cold leftovers his mother packed for him, and he'd wander farther and farther from the school grounds. Sometimes the crows would see him, and he'd throw them pieces of Korean barbecued beef, the fat congealed white and cold. They'd swarm down and fight for it. Then they'd follow him, flying from telephone pole to telephone pole, watching and waiting.

As Mira and Lenny walk along side streets he spots someone from his grade, Frankie, a hulking overweight slob who picks on the younger kids. He munches a bag of Doritos while walking, and when he sees them he holds the bag in his mouth and pulls his eyes slanted. He yells with the bag still in his teeth, "Ching chong chinaman!"

Mira turns to Lenny, who shakes his head and continues walking. Frankie yells it again, but this time drops his bag of Doritos, the chips spreading across the sidewalk, and he curses. Mira laughs. Frankie looks up venomously.

Lenny whispers to his sister to shut up and keep walking.

Frankie yells to Lenny, "You're gonna pay for that!"

Mira looks confused. "Why do you have to pay for that?"

Lenny yanks her along, saying, "You just got me in trouble."

"Oh."

"Now he's going to pick on me."

"I didn't know!" she cries.

"Come on."

She follows him home contritely.

Lenny practices saying, "Sally sells seashells at the seashore," muttering to himself while trying to keep the leakage down.

"What?" Mira asks.

He repeats it quietly.

"Who's Sally? What are you talking about?"

He looks directly at her and says, "Sally sells seashells at the seashore."

Mira sighs. "You're weird."

Sweets 'N Gifts is on Merrick Road, a busy highway with no bike lane, so Lenny has to ride on the sidewalk. A mix of storefronts and office buildings line the street, and he weaves around annoyed pedestrians. Twenty minutes later he approaches his mother's store, which looks very out of place nestled between the Emerald Bar and Carpets for Less. A large hardware depot looms nearby, and most of the other businesses here—a linoleum and flooring outlet, a mattress store—are connected to home and building supplies.

Lenny drops his bicycle in front of the store and walks in, a small bell ringing. His mother leans on the front counter, reading a large annotated bible. She looks up, startled. "Lenny?" she asks. "What are you doing here?"

"Visiting."

"You rode all the way here?"

He nods and looks around. She has added more jewelry in the front display cases, silver and jade earrings and necklaces and small jewelry boxes sit on shelves next to silver seagull mobiles and figurines. The collection is eclectic and puzzling to Lenny, since the jars of candy lined up behind the counter have nothing to do with jewelry, and customers who want one wouldn't really want the other. He stares at the mobiles hanging near the front. The afternoon sun shines through the tinted front window and hits the sparkling stars.

"Do you want some candy?" she asks.

Strangely enough he doesn't. When the store first opened, Lenny tried the different varieties, but he preferred sour candies, which she doesn't carry. His brother and sister like the myriad of chocolates, but Lenny doesn't seem to have the same sweet tooth. He takes a sweet rock candy just because he might regret later not having something.

She shows him the alarm button, just a doorbell button under the counter that buzzes the carpet store next door in case of an emergency. Without thinking, Lenny presses it. Lenny's mother yells, "Don't!" and he jumps away. She turns to the door, waiting. She explains that the owner is supposed to come here to help her if she buzzes.

But after a few minutes of silence, she wonders aloud if he didn't hear it. She tells him to go play in back, and never to press the button again. Lenny wanders past the shelves along the walls, more wiry desk mobiles with glittering gulls rocking and swaying.

He pushes through a beaded curtain and stops at the sight of the back closet. A folding chair from their kitchen stands by the door. This must have been the chair the robber had used to trap his mother in the closet. Lenny peers out through the beaded curtain and sees her checking the panic button, following the wire along the counter and into the wall.

She turns and says to him, "I think it's okay."

"You were in the back closet?"

She nods her head. "Your father wants me to have a gun here."

Lenny wonders if his father has a gun at the house. "Are you going to?" he asks.

"No."

"Does he have a gun?"

"Your father used to be a soldier. Didn't you know that?"

"The navy."

She looks at him for a moment, and says, "He was a commando."

"What's that?"

She tells him the story: Not too long ago, when they had gone to the Korean church in Flushing, Queens, a man took her aside and asked if she knew who her husband was. "Who my husband is?" she asked. "Of course I do." "No, who your husband was," he replied. She wasn't sure what he was talking about, but he explained that he was a former commando with the South Korean Navy. He had recognized her husband. Umee, suddenly understanding that something bad was about to come out of this man's mouth, didn't want to know anything and stopped him. Later, though, as she kept thinking about it, imagining all kinds of possibilities, she had to know. She looked up the man in the church directory and called the man's wife. Then, after talking with him, she learned that her husband Yul was infamous. He had been in the special forces, in an elite commando unit that interrogated enemy soldiers. Yul outshined everyone in his unit, but he had a reputation for cruelty, especially for murdering the prisoners.

Lenny listens to this story, incredulous. "Dad?" he asks.

She replies, "Other soldiers knew about him and were scared of him."

"Really?"

She nods her head. She studies him, waiting for more of a reaction.

Lenny asks, "How many people did he kill?"

"I don't know. I think many."

The fact is that Lenny can easily imagine his father shooting someone. He had once seen his father look coldly at his mother and smack her in the face without blinking. Lenny was only five years old, maybe even younger, and the brutality of the act hadn't surprised him as much as the efficiency and speed, and how emotionless his father had seemed.

"Does he know martial arts?" Lenny asks.

"Maybe," she replies. "Do you want to stay a while? I can drive you."

"I have to practice."

"You're going to ride your bike all the way home?"

"It's not far," he says, seeing the open bible on the counter. He knows she's bored and lonely, but there isn't much for him to do here. He walks toward the door, and she asks him what he wants for dinner. "Anything you want," she says.

"*Bibimbap.*" It's a mixed rice, vegetable and beef dish.

"Okay!" she says. She waves to him as he leaves the store, the bell on the handle jangling.

As he rides home, he keeps thinking about his father as a killer.

9

This is what Lenny knows about his father, Yul: Raised in a turbulent household in North Korea before the Communist takeover, Yul was the second of four children—he had three sisters and a brother. Yul's father was, among other things, a drug smuggler who often disappeared for weeks, and sometimes Yul would have to track him down.

Yul once told the family a story about how his father had made an opium run into China, and Yul, only a teen, had to sneak into China to find him. Yul's mother had ordered him to bring his father back. Yul eventually found his father and helped him smuggle opium back into Korea.

Lenny learns from his mother that Yul and his brother had been beaten by their father, and had a miserable childhood. Yul's younger brother confirmed this once when he visited, and told Umee how they used to have chores on the farm that often kept them working ten hours a day. When the war broke out, Yul ran away from home and enlisted in the South Korean Navy by lying about his age. His family escaped to the south, but he didn't stay very close to them. After the war he emigrated to the U.S. on a student visa to study computers and finance, and married Ed's mother. After she abandoned both of them, he sent Ed to Korea, to stay for more than four years. When he married Umee, Ed returned to the states and Umee accepted him as her own. Lenny was born a couple of years later.

Lenny has a trail of clues that confirms bits and pieces of his father's history. The pucker wound on his leg is supposedly an old football injury, but now Lenny is certain it's a bullet wound. He first noticed the scarred hole on his father's thigh when he watched his father mow the lawn, and when he asked about it Yul explained that someone had kicked him during a football game. But a kick, no matter how violent, wouldn't give someone a pucker scar like that.

That Yul has a military background is obvious. On weekend mornings he awakens the family by opening all the windows, even in the winter, barking at them that they need the fresh morning air. If he had a bugle they would undoubtedly have morning reveille.

He keeps his shoes meticulously polished and lined up in his closet. He teaches Ed and Lenny the intricate method of shoe shining—the proper stages of brushing, cleaning and polishing—and occasionally slips them a few dollars to shine his shoes for him, as long as their work "passes inspection."

And he's obsessed with his children being weak. This seems to be a fault far worse than any other, even being lazy, of which he often accuses Ed. Weakness is unpardonable. Physical, mental and emotional weakness are all related, in his estimation, and despite being a child, Lenny isn't allowed to show any kind of frailty.

One summer evening Lenny whines about the water being too cold at Newbridge Pool. Yul says Lenny should be able to take it, and he orders Lenny in. Afterwards Lenny complains about the shower being too hot, and his father whips the towel at him and says he's too babied. He needs to be tougher. This only makes Lenny whine louder. When he almost throws a tantrum, his father tells the rest of the family they will be leaving without Lenny.

Lenny has only his bathing suit and flip-flops. His father grabs his bag and leaves the pool. When Lenny tries to follow his father pushes him back, and says, "You act like a baby. You learn to take care of yourself."

Lenny watches from the gate. His father orders the rest of the family into the white Dodge Dart, and Mira keeps looking back in confusion. He sees her asking their mother, "What about Lenny?" But they climb into the car. Umee yells at Yul, but they drive away. Mira presses her face against the rear window, looking back in alarm. Lenny sits down near the gate, not sure what he is supposed to do. He doesn't even have his street clothes with him.

It's getting cold. Lenny wraps himself in the towel and huddles on a chair, suddenly hungry. Families begin packing up and leaving, and only a few groups of teens are still in the water. The night lights flicker on, the pool glowing. Lenny stares up at a large bug zapper near one of the lights—the sparks fascinate him, since he knows the bugs are being electrocuted. After a while he walks back to the gate, expecting someone to be waiting, but no one is there. It takes about an hour for him to realize that his father was serious. He wonders where he will sleep. A few families eat in the food court, the smell of burgers and fries making him hungrier.

After two hours he walks back into the quiet and empty locker rooms and takes a long, hot shower. He considers sleeping here overnight, and then walking home in the morning. It's about seven miles back to the house, and he isn't sure he can make it in his flip-flops, definitely not at night, definitely not in his bathing suit. The logistics of survival begin to overwhelm him. He dries off and looks for clothes to steal, but there aren't any. He needs dinner. He walks back out to the food court and stares at the counter where a teenaged girl with a red and white paper hat prepares a hot dog for a customer. He wraps his towel tightly around his shoulders, and moves closer to a heat lamp, the glowing red coils humming. He can't stop shivering.

The girl behind the counter sees him and motions him over. She has acne all over her cheeks. Without saying anything she throws him a bag of potato chips.

"I don't have any money," he tells her.

She smiles, put her finger to her lips, and winks. She turns to a customer, and Lenny stares at his small bag of chips, amazed by this act of kindness. Then he tears into it and tries to eat too fast, the chips cutting his mouth.

"Lenny?" his mother calls.

He turns. She carries her straw beach bag and is wearing a sweatshirt. She waves him over, and he runs to her, his flip-flops slapping the cement.

"Are you okay?" she asks, taking him into her arms.

He is so relieved that he buries his face in her sweatshirt and sobs.

10

Her sweatshirt is soft. Soft and warm. The contrast with the cold air, the smell of chlorine and sunscreen, the stinging salt of the potato chips on his chapped lips—all of these remain vivid in his memory, and he's certain it's because of the uniqueness of the experience, the distress imprinting every detail so that all he has to do is smell chlorine and remember everything.

Perhaps his father's connection to the Navy and his obsession with weakness makes most of Lenny's early experiences with water traumatic. Yul tries to teach Lenny to swim by throwing him off a dock and into a lake in Upstate New York. He watches Lenny thrash and panic, and Lenny yells for help, but Yul just says, "Swim."

Lenny sinks. He stops thrashing. He looks up and sees the wavy, blurry blue sky through the water, and his father's silhouette leaning over. He knows enough to hold his breath, but not enough to paddle. As he sinks deeper down he thinks, It's so quiet.

Then his father jumps in and pulls him out, sighing. He lifts Lenny up onto the dock, where he curls up and shivers. He breathes deeply. He's confused by the whole experience. Yul stares at him, puzzled, almost incredulous, as he says, "You don't have a survival instinct."

In his own warped way he is trying to prepare his children for the harshness of the world as he knows it, and has the drill sergeant's mentality of instilling discipline, though it's hard for any of his children to respect his authority since he is so obviously undisciplined himself—an alcoholic and wife-beater rarely instills much confidence.

However, after Lenny learns of his father's military background, he understands him better. Lenny researches at the Merrick Library what Navy commandos do. He learns that they are highly trained fighters who infiltrate enemy territory and dive and plant bombs underwater. He also reads about commandos knowing close-quarters, hand-to-hand combat, and becomes convinced that his father must know martial arts.

His father has seen the kung-fu books, and he has watched Lenny train on weekends in the back yard, but he never says anything. Not too long after Lenny learns about his father's military background, and while Lenny practices his kicks in the back yard, his father walks out and watches him. Lenny asks him if he knows tae kwon do.

His father says he doesn't.

"Didn't you learn it in Korea as a kid?"

He shakes his head. "Tae kwon do is Japanese k-k-karate made K-Korean. It d-didn't happen until I was in the Navy." His stutter is particularly bad during quieter moments like these, the hard consonants elongating and stumbling.

"What did you learn in the Navy?"

He says, "Self-defense."

"Martial arts?"

"Judo."

"Can you show me?"

"You want me to show you judo?"

Lenny nods his head.

His father puts down his drink and says, "I will show

you one move. It's a basic flip. Come here."

He approaches, knowing that his father only had one or two glasses, so is okay. Yul tells his son that he will use Lenny's own movements to help take him down. He says, "Come at me."

"How?"

"Like you want to grab me or push me."

Lenny steps forward. His father yanks him closer, pulling him off-balance, and then everything suddenly spins over him. Lenny lands on the grass with a thump, but his father cushions the fall with his arm. He lets Lenny go and stands over him. "You see how I use your force to flip you?"

He pulls Lenny up, and laughs when Lenny staggers back, dizzy. He then shows Lenny how to pivot his body, thrust his hip out, and pull an opponent over his hip and onto the ground. When he tells Lenny to try it on him, Lenny says, "You're too big."

"The bigger your opponent, the more momentum he has. Try." His father moves toward him and grabs his shoulders, pushing. Lenny steps back, pulls his father forward, and turns. His father then lets Lenny flip him over his hip, and his father lands on the grass.

He stands up slowly, brushing off his jeans. He then pats Lenny's head and says, "Good job."

Lenny turns to the house, and notices his mother watching anxiously. When she sees that he's okay she smiles and disappears into the kitchen.

His father picks up his drink and sits on the rickety patio chair, propping his feet on a picnic bench. He watches Lenny continue practicing his martial arts.

He asks, "You really want to learn tae kwon do?"

"Yes."

"They teach it at Korean churches. Maybe we all go tomorrow."

Lenny asks if he would have to go to bible study.

"Yes. You have to take Korean language lessons too."

"I don't know any Korean."

"That is why you take lessons."

All that matters to Lenny is the tae kwon do, so he agrees.
He hurries back to his room to study up on tae kwon do
terms.

That night he listens to *The Five Deadly Venoms* on the
small cassette tape recorder, the large white earpiece chafing
his ear canal. Since he recorded the movie simply by placing
the recorder next to the TV, it also picked up his sister asking
him what he was doing, and his shushing her. Lenny memorized most of the dialogue and can envision the scenes as
the story unfolds in his ear, the cheesy sound effects even
cheesier when isolated from the screen. But he mouths the
words of his favorite character, the Scorpian.

In his other ear he hears his parents fighting. Even though
he doesn't know the Korean language, he seems to be able to
understand bits and pieces of the fight, especially when the
occasional English word is dropped in, like "store" or "tax-
es." They are arguing about the store losing money, about
the robbery, and about going to church. The fight isn't a bad
one, because his mother seems to get a concession, although
Lenny isn't sure what that is. They withdraw to different
parts of the house—his father in the living room, his mother
in the bedroom—and the house becomes oddly quiet.

His mother reads the bible, his father plays classical records on the stereo, his sister writes her book, his brother

is out with his friends, and Lenny listens to the static-filled tape of a badly dubbed kung-fu flick. It's a normal Saturday night.

PART II

The Deal

11

Lenny understands that his father has had a hard life, including a traumatic stint in the Korean War and financial and familial pressures in the U.S., and he knows his father is profoundly unhappy. During a quieter moment his father tells Lenny of his dream to own a large sailboat and sail around the world.

Yul sits on the front steps drinking a whiskey and ice, the glass sweating and leaving a dark ring on the bricks. His face is flushed, his eyelids heavy. The muggy heat of an unseasonable spring afternoon eases away as the sun sets and the fireflies begin to glimmer. Lenny returns home from the movies, and sees his father sipping his drink and watching the cars drive by. He sits with his shoulders hunched and he sways forward and back. He looks up as Lenny approaches and asks where he's been. Lenny tells him. His father then begins talking to him as if continuing a conversation, and he says that the boat has to be junked. Lenny realizes he's talking about an old sixteen-foot boat he bought and docked in Freeport. During a fierce storm a couple of weeks ago, the boat, which his father had tied up too close to the dock, was swamped. His father says there's too much water damage to repair it.

Lenny knows the boat is another source of contention between his parents, since it was more than they could afford and the docking fees have been adding up, but Lenny also knows his mother didn't fight this as hard as she could have. She told him that having a boat had always been a dream of his father's, and although he preferred a large sailboat, his sixteen-footer with an outboard engine was good enough for now.

Lenny has only been on the boat once, on a family outing shortly after he and his brother repainted the hull. His mother felt nauseated, which annoyed his father, and Lenny didn't understand the point of having a boat. He asked Ed where they were going, and when Ed told him that that had no real destination, Lenny felt like that it was a waste of time.

When his father tells him about losing this boat Lenny asks him if he's going to get another one. His father looks up at him, almost startled to hear him speak. Yul thinks about it and shakes his head. He says that when he was Lenny's age all he dreamed about was getting away from home and sailing around the world. He wanted to see so many things. That was why he ran away and joined the Navy. He says, "I was happy when I was out at sea."

Lenny asks him why. He tells his son he wants to see the world, and to live on a sailboat and travel from port to port is the best way to do this. This is the first time Lenny has ever heard him utter anything close to a dream, and it surprises him. He begins to realize how stifling it must have been for him to live in the suburbs, commuting two hours a day into Manhattan, chained to a mortgage and a family.

There are definitely some things Lenny appreciates about his father. That he directs Lenny to a Korean church is his attempt to help, and he also offers another brief lesson in judo, showing Lenny how to fall back and flip an attacker over him. This particular move is useful when Frankie harasses Lenny one morning as he walks to school.

Lenny sees Frankie in the distance, his jeans too large and slipping down his waist. He yanks them up as he moves sloppily across the street, his book bag jostling, his stomach jiggling, and he calls out loudly to Lenny that he owes him for his chips.

A few kids from their class approach. Frankie sees them and pushes Lenny. He says, "You going to pay me back or what?"

"I didn't do anything," Lenny replies, his voice whiney.

Frankie curls his lip. "Speak English, Chinaman. What'd you say?"

Lenny remembers his speech exercises—Sally sells seashells at the seashore. "I did not do anything," he says more slowly, concentrating.

"Are you retard or something? Give me my money."

Frankie moves closer, intending to push Lenny again, but this time, remembering his father's lesson, he grabs Frankie's arms, pulls him off balance, and falls back on the ground, rolling him onto Lenny's feet and kicking him over and onto the sidewalk. Frankie is heavy, but because of the momentum Lenny sends him sprawling onto the concrete. Frankie howls in pain. Lenny jumps up, steps forward and kicks him in the ribs. Frankie starts to cry.

Lenny kicks him again, hard, and then backs away. The three other kids across the street watch this. One of them says, "He knows kung-fu!"

Frankie's elbow bleeds, his books fluttering across the sidewalk, and he curls up to hold his ribs. "I'm telling on you!" he cries. "I'm telling!"

Knowing that the other kids are still watching, Lenny says, "If you tell, I'll kill you." He then does a kung-fu salute he learned from imitating the movies—fist and open-hand coming together, and a slight bow. He walks away, Frankie still crying, and the other kids whispering how Lenny must be a kung-fu master.

The news spreads quickly, and by mid-day, when he joins the other "walker" students filing out of the school to head home for lunch, he notices a few kids talking to each other and glancing at him. One comes up to him and asks, "What degree black belt are you?"

"What?" Lenny replies, not sure what he means.

"I heard what you did to Frankie. What kind of black belt are you?"

Lenny replies that he isn't any belt. "In my school we don't give out belts."

"Is it kung-fu?"

"A mix of kung-fu, judo, and tae kwon do."

"Cool. Just wondering," the boy says and reports back to his friends.

The teacher's aide opens the door and waves them out. She doesn't check for their passes, and since Lenny doesn't have one he always expects to get caught. But she recognizes him, and greets him with a smile and a nod of a head.

It's spring and the trees are beginning to sprout green, the dogwoods to bloom, and dandelions to pop up on the manicured lawns. Lenny's mother packed him a cold *mandu* sandwich—leftover dumplings squashed in between two soggy slices of bread with ketchup—and juice box and a Twinkie. He bites into the sandwich, which tastes good but the soggy bread crumbles in his hands. He feeds the crows.

The flush of his new notoriety elates him. He wonders what else his father could teach him. The judo flip worked flawlessly, and he's now more convinced of his father's commando background.

Walking a different route, he passes a strip mall on Merrick Road and sees a row of pay phones. He still has another thirty minutes before lunch period ends, so he makes a collect call to another number close to his own.

When the operator asks for his name, he tells her, "Frankie Williams."

The woman on the other line asks, "Frankie who?"

"Williams," he replies.

The woman laughs. It's a delicate, tickling laugh, and she says, "Sure, I'll accept the charges."

This catches him off-guard, and when the operator tells him to go ahead, he stutters with, "Uh, hello."

The woman says, "Well, Frankie Williams, you sound pretty young. Do you do this a lot, make collect calls?"

"Not really."

"Is that your real name?"

"No."

"My name is Nancy. What's yours?"

"Lenny."

"Well, Lenny, do your parents know you do this? Why aren't you in school?"

"Lunch period."

"Lenny, you sound like a sweet kid. Maybe you should be more constructive with your time. Do you know what I mean?"

"No."

"Read a book. Play sports. Study. Okay? If you want to

call me again, you can, but don't call collect."

"Really?"

"Sure, why not? Do you remember my number?"

"Kind of."

She repeats her number, and then says, "Be good. No more collect calls, okay?"

"Okay."

She hangs up, and Lenny recites her number aloud a few times. He decides to have a crush on her.

12

The Valley Stream Methodist Church sits near a freeway, a steep driveway descending into a narrow parking lot with a view of the small cemetery, tombstones propped up in front of the parking spaces. The church has an American congregation that finishes at eleven, and when Lenny's family arrives in the middle of the shift change, they see the Caucasian churchgoers in their Sunday suits and dresses climbing into their cars as the black-haired Korean congregation begins filtering in.

His parents head to the main worship service, while Lenny and Mira walk tentatively into the children's service upstairs. Ed conveniently disappeared earlier in the morning.

A few Korean American kids stare at Lenny and his sister as they take their seats in the back. The young woman with thick eyeglasses at the front of the room speaks in English with a heavy Korean accent, and Lenny has trouble understanding her. She switches to Korean, and he's completely lost.

Then a boy with a crew cut stands up and begins reciting something in Korean. Mira looks at Lenny, puzzled. He shrugs his shoulders. When the boy finishes, he sits down and a girl next to him wearing a white and blue summer dress stands up and recites the same thing. This continues down the row, and Lenny realizes that everyone seems to know this. He turns back to the doorway, wondering if he can leave without attracting attention.

Mira whispers, "What are they doing?"

"I think they memorized a bible quote."

She looks stricken, her face turning pale. A few of the kids stumble with the memorization, but everyone has to speak. Mira becomes more anxious as her turn approaches. She balls her hands into small fists and presses them into her thighs. The girl next to her stands up and recites the quote flawlessly.

When it's Mira's turn she looks to Lenny desperately. He stands up and tells the teacher, "My sister and I are just visiting today."

The teacher asks something in Korean.

He shakes his head. "We don't speak it. We're just visiting."

"Can you say the Lord's Prayer in Korean?" she asks.

"No."

"Can you say it in English?"

Even though Lenny once learned it at the Sunday school across the street from his house, his mind blanks. "We're just visiting. Let the next people go."

He sits down. Everyone stares. He turns to the boy next to him and says, "You go."

The boy stands up and recites the prayer in sing-song Korean.

After this ordeal, Lenny is eager to start the tae kwon do practice, but everyone is then shepherded into their Korean language classes, and because Mira and Lenny know nothing, they are placed in the Kindergarten section in the kiddie room, the chairs and table miniaturized so he sits uncomfortably with his knees up to his chin. The kindergartners look at him with confusion.

Lenny doesn't even know the alphabet, and when the other kids read out the letters, he feels stupid. Mira seems to catch on quickly, imitating the others and connecting the sounds with the consonants after only a few minutes.

Lenny becomes annoyed with her, and glares at her when she recites the consonants after only two prompts by the teacher.

The class lasts for forty-five minutes, and the only thing he learns is how little he knows. The teacher gives him a workbook to practice, but he has already decided he isn't coming back.

He leaves the class in a hurry, and finds that the main church service has finished. His parents are downstairs at a buffet lunch, platters of Korean dishes laid out on long tables. Dozens of conversations in Korean fill the basement auditorium, the clanking of chopsticks mingling with the sounds of rice cookers whistling steam. A woman announces something on the loudspeaker, and Lenny recognizes the word "tae kwon do." Some of the parents shoo their children, and the girls file out toward the basement, while the boys walk out of the church. Lenny turns to his mother, who motions for him to follow the boys.

They walk along the cemetery to a small white building that has an open, dusty hardwood floor with folding chairs stacked to one side. It looks as if funeral services are held here: a podium stands next a large, low platform near the front that can only be for a casket. Next to the podium is a small, balding Korean man in a tae kwon do uniform with a black belt. His scalp glistens. The lapels have red and black embroidered Korean lettering, and a dragon on the left sleeve. Lenny is greatly impressed. The man yells at them in Korean, and the other kids quickly begin changing into their gi's.

Lenny approaches the teacher, who looks him up and down, and not knowing what to do, Lenny bows.

The teacher speaks to him in Korean, but Lenny shakes his head. The teacher sighs. In English he tells Lenny to follow along as best he can. "Have you studied tae kwon do before?"

"From books."

The teacher frowns and motions him to move to the back row. Almost everyone is a white belt, but there are a few yellow and greens. Lenny is the only one in jeans. The teacher begins yelling out warm-up exercises, and Lenny follows along. Then they move on to punches and blocks. When the teacher demonstrates the punches, his uniform snaps loudly from the force. He yells for them to feel the air explode from their punches. Their bare feet slide and thump over the dirty floor, their yells bouncing off the high ceilings. Lenny notices the other kids' feet are blackened, and then looks down in surprise at his own black feet.

After a sequence of kicks, the teacher stops everyone. He looks at Lenny, and says in English, "Do that again."

Lenny does the side kick, and the teacher walks over to him and tells him to turn his body more. Lenny tries, but the teacher grabs his shoulders to keep from pivoting.

"Where did you learn that?" the teacher asks.

"From a book."

"The form is all wrong. You must forget everything you learned and start over."

Some of the other kids snicker. Lenny's face heats up, and when the teacher orders him to try the kick again, his foot slips on the dusty floor, and he falls to the ground, banging his elbow. Everyone laughs.

The teacher says, "No more books."

He walks to the front of the class. Lenny pulls himself up, shaking, and tries to get through the rest of the practice.

That night he checks his book and looks at his form in the mirror. He then tries it the teacher's way, but it doesn't feel right. He hears his father yelling at Ed for disappearing this morning. Ed yells back, "I can do what I want!"

Their father bellows in a deep and angry voice, "Ungrateful boy!" and there's a smack. Ed cries out. There's the sound of a scuffle, and then the screen door slams. Outside, Ed yells "You're crazy! I can't wait to get out of here!"

Lenny runs to the window and sees his brother holding his cheek, his eyes murderous, as he storms away.

His father curses in Korean.

His mother murmurs something, and his father barks at her.

Lenny returns to his tae kwon do book, and after studying it for a while he throws it across the room, angry that the practice was such a failure. Lenny had fantasies of excelling, of his self-teaching somehow making him better than the others, and now he doesn't want to return. They had all laughed at him, and the memory of this sears. He wonders if the teacher focused on him because he was new and can't speak Korean.

Lenny's mother checks on him, and she says in a weak, tired voice that she's going to bed early. Her face is pale and drawn, but she smiles and asks if he had a good day at church.

"No," he replies. "I don't like it. I don't want to go back."

"Your sister had a good time."

"I didn't."

She tells him to get ready for bed, because of school tomorrow. He realizes that he forgot to do a school project—a presentation on a current events topic. There are no newspapers in the house, and it's too late to go to the store. This will be the third project he'll miss, and his teacher, Mrs. Trilly, had said she would write his parents a note if it happened again. He decides to buy a newspaper first thing in the morning and write up the report before class.

He puts in a different cassette tonight—*Drunken Master*—and falls asleep to the lull of fighting sound effects, reminding him of the tae kwon do teacher's punches. But the tape sounds better than the real thing.

13

Late at night Lenny finds his mother studying her large annotated bible at the kitchen table. The gilded pages glint under the lights, and a thick velvet bookmark hangs limply over the side. She sips from a mug of ginseng tea, tendrils of steam rising up. She turns to him, bleary-eyed, and asks him why he's up.

"I can't sleep," he tells her as he sits down at the table. She asks if he wants anything to drink, but he says he's okay. They sit quietly for a while. The plaid vinyl tablecloth has intricate patterns that occupy him. He traces the lines with his fingernail.

"Do you remember when I used to tell you stories?" she asks.

"About Korea."

"They helped you sleep. Do you want to hear them?"

"Not yet. Why are you awake?"

She studies him, and tells him about her doctor's visit. She has been losing weight, feeling tired all the time, and looks thin and sickly. Finally, after a few weeks of this she went to the doctor, who diagnosed her with anemia, and prescribed iron pills. But he also found some irregularities with her thyroid, and wanted her to come in for more tests. She sips her tea and adds that her older sister died from breast cancer, her father from leukemia, and one of her two brothers died from lung cancer. "It's just me and your uncle Jimmy."

She rubs her throat. "I will be fine, but just in case, you have to promise me you will always take care of your sister."

"In case of what?"

"In case anything happens to me."

Lenny remains still. She sees his uneasiness, and says quickly, "Just promise me. Nothing will happen, but I need to know you and Mira will be okay."

"All right," he says, but has no idea how he would take care of his sister. "Does it hurt? Your throat?"

"No. It's just swollen." She explains that she might have a tumor on her thyroid gland, but the doctor doesn't think her anemia is related to that. "I just need more iron."

She tells him to go to sleep. "Come." She leads him out of the kitchen and to his bedroom, where she tucks him in and sits on the corner of his bed. "What story do you want to hear?"

"The one with the bear and the tiger."

She laughs quietly. "Again?" She whispers it to him: There was a she-bear and a tiger who prayed fervently to become humans. To test their resolve, their god told them to stay in their cave for one hundred days, eating only roots and garlic, and only then would they become human. So they did this. The tiger became more and more restless, however, while the she-bear sat quietly. After many days the tiger couldn't stay in the cave any longer and ran away. The she-bear continued to wait without complaining. After the hundred days passed, the god turned her into a beautiful woman. The god then turned himself into a human and married her. They soon had a son who became king of Korea, and ruled the land for fifteen hundred peaceful years.

14

The fight begins over Yul buying a beat-up old Cadillac. He and Umee share the Dodge Dart, and since he commutes by train, they need only one car.

One afternoon, though, he comes home early from work in a huge Cadillac, the blue paint dull and the vinyl top gray with dirt. The chrome bumpers are rusted, and the exhaust puffs smoke whenever he accelerates. Mira and Lenny hurry to the front window when they hear it pull into the driveway and their mother stands behind them as their father climbs out. She exhales sharply and says something in Korean. She puts on her slippers and runs outside.

Lenny watches them argue, his father pointing to the Cadillac and then to the Dodge in the garage, and the issue is obviously money. His mother storms back into the house, muttering, and his father begins washing and waxing his new car. She says to Lenny, "He wasted an entire paycheck on that car!" She retreats to the bedroom, fuming.

His father comes in, wanting to show off his new Cadillac, and he says, "This is the high-class car of America."

Mira and Lenny walk out and stare at the car, which seems enormous compared to the Dodge. A closer look reveals the torn upholstery and patches of rust along the bottom of the doors. Lenny isn't sure how much one paycheck is, but even to his young eyes he thinks this is a piece of junk. His brother's friends are car buffs, so he often sees shiny Corvettes and Mustangs picking Ed up, and those deep-throated rum-

blings from the engines sounds healthy and vibrant compared to the Cadillac's wheezing and coughing.

When they return inside, their parents continue fighting.
His mother says something in Korean, and from the tone
Lenny knows it's something along the lines of the unfair-
ness of his purchase. Her voice shakes with anger, and she
tells Mira and Lenny to go out and play.

Their father slams his hand against the door. He curses
in Korean.

Mira and Lenny hurry outside as their father bellows in
his deep, booming voice.

They walk across the street to the Presbyterian church,
and head to the small playground in the back, a warped
slide and monkey bars covered in spiderwebs sitting in
rocky dirt. On the other side of the small lot is a spinning
platform that gets Mira sick, and two rocking seahorses on
large springs.

Tall thick trees shroud the back of the church, the sun
setting and casting an orange glow over everything. The
red brick seems brown, even black, in the shadows, with the
white trim dirty and speckled with spots of peeling paint.
The lights above the back door flicker on, and Lenny notices
movement inside. Some kind of meeting is going on in one
of the back rooms, the fluorescent lighting shining yellow
out the windows. When the meeting ends and the dozen or
so men and women file out the back and to their cars in the
adjacent lot, Lenny sees that the back door to the church is
loose, the last woman leaving having trouble with the lock.
The two doors rattle closed, and the woman has to push one
door into the other for the lock to engage.

Once all the cars drive off Lenny walks to the rear doors

and pushes. They're still loose. He peers down through the crack and sees the bolt engaged. When he pulls on one door he yanks it free from the bolt, and the door swings open.

Mira climbs down from the monkey bars. "What are you doing?" she asks.

He turns to her. "Want to go exploring?"

The church at dusk is eerily quiet. Mira bumps into him trying to stay close, and he has to resist scaring her with stories about ghosts or demons. He once told her about the devil, and because of the bible stories she's heard from Sunday school, she's terrified of anything linked to Hell.

They walk through the back halls, the linoleum floors reflecting the shadowy orange light outside, and into the main worship area, the pulpit dark and quiet, smelling of pine oil. The carpet dampens all sounds. The pews have a red glow from an emergency exit sign. The dim red glow spreads over them as they approach the choir section and look up at the stained glass windows, where only a part of the reds and blues are lit from the setting sun. They catch the last bits of sunlight as the room darkens, and Mira says, "It's spooky here."

Lenny walks up to the pulpit and stands behind it, looking out over the pews. His sister moves to the choir section, leafing through the hymnal and sheet music. Behind the pulpit Lenny finds an empty, smudged water glass, a bible, and a tangle of microphone wires. In the bible are a few sheets of paper, drafts of a sermon with the typed text edited and scribbled over. It surprises him that the minister would read from a messy copy.

"I could sing," Mira says.

"Go ahead."

"No music."

The organ sits beside her, but neither of them know how to turn it on. They'd both had piano lessons, though Mira seems to prefer the viola. They walk beyond the organ and find a narrow doorway in back, almost a secret passageway because the door is hidden in the ornate woodwork. "It's so they can sneak in and out without the congregation seeing," he tells her.

They follow the dark hallway down a few steps and emerge into another hall that opens up to a small office. One of the windows look out the front of the church, and they have a direct view of their house. The large front living room window is lit up. They see their parents still fighting.

Mira says, "It's getting dark."

"Scared?"

"I don't want to get in trouble."

He leads her back through the narrow hallway and to the rear exit. Now that he knows how to break in here, he wants to explore the church on his own.

When they return to the house Mira immediately goes to her room, while the fight in the living room escalates. His father chases his mother, who screams. Lenny stays in the kitchen as they tumble into a wall in the dining area. When he peers around the corner he sees his father choking his mother up against the wall. He has one hand on her throat, the other hand drawn back in a fist. She clutches at his arm, gagging, and kicks his leg, which makes him grunt and tighten his grip.

Then Yul turns and sees Lenny. He lets go of Umee's

throat and orders Lenny to his room. Lenny's mother bends over and gasps for air. She waves him away. Lenny quickly retreats to his bedroom and listens to the fight continue.

15

When Ed learns that he was rejected from all the Ivy League colleges he applied to, but was accepted to the New York state schools, their father is so cruel that even Mira understands the dynamics and turns to Ed in sympathy. They sit mutely through dinner—meatloaf and vegetables piled onto the platters, a large foamy beer in front of their father. They eat in the breakfast nook by the kitchen, and the small radio on top of a shelf plays classical music. Their father tells all of them that he will not pay for his children to go to bad schools. He says to Ed, "Why should I waste my money on a stupid boy?"

Umee snaps at him in Korean, and he turns to Lenny. "You get good grades and go to a good school or you will be a garbage man like your stupid brother."

He then says to Umee in English, "I warned him that I would not p-p-pay for bad schools. I told him years ago! Did he study and work hard? No!"

He then tells a familiar story, how he had to sell apples on the streets to make money, and how he had gone to the Korean Naval Academy and became one of the youngest officers in Korean history. He then was accepted to graduate school in the U.S. on a scholarship, and his children are all so soft and lucky to have everything handed to them. As he tells this he uses the same hand motions for emphasis, a stabbing finger aimed at Ed, and his normally stoic expression becomes more animated, his cheeks red and his eyes flashing.

"I can't take this," Ed says, and leaves the table.

"I did not excuse you!"

Ed says something under his breath, grabbing his jeans jacket, and walks out the back door. Yul then lectures Lenny and Mira about the importance of education and studying hard. He says, "Look at me. I am a professional b-b-businessman."

Lenny sees his mother frown.

Later that night when Lenny finds his mother doing a crossword puzzle in the kitchen, he asks her about the tests with the doctor.

"I go this weekend. And your father and I are closing the store soon."

"The candy store? Why?"

She sighs. "If your father loses his job we can't keep losing money with the store. I might have to get a job too."

"Is he going to get fired?"

She shrugs her shoulders. She studies him, and then walks to kitchen counter and shows him a yellow legal pad with scribbled notes. She says, "Your father was supposed to write a report. He made me write it, and then he handed it in like this."

Lenny skims the pages. His father had written in broken English, his script messy, and Lenny makes out a few lines that read "transfer data from lupe tape to cartige tape…" He stares at the words, and asks, "What's lupe?"

"L-o-o-p."

"He spelled it wrong?" Lenny says, shocked.

"And didn't type it. He also made some big mistakes with backing up something, and they lost a lot of information."

Lenny stares at his father's handwriting, and is amazed by this. Even as a kid he knows to type something up and check the spelling. "That's why he's in trouble," he says.

"He's already looking for a new job."

"Why is he so mean to Ed?"

"Maybe because your brother reminds him of himself too much."

"He's not going to pay for Ed's college?"

"You don't worry. When you go to college I will help pay for it."

College seems far away, but the idea of it already burdens him. "How much does it cost?"

"Ivy League schools can be twenty thousand dollars a year."

This amount, twenty thousand, would slowly begin to obsess him. Lenny is a worrier, and has already begun grinding his teeth at night, with headaches and a sore jaw in the mornings. He learned what he was doing only after his mother heard him once and woke him up. She told him that it sounded as if he were chewing on rocks.

His mother said that if he did well in school, a scholarship could pay for tuition, and she could always take out loans. Up until then Lenny has never taken school seriously—it's easy and routine, and his grades are average. He begins wondering if he should pay more attention.

So when he goes to school the next day he feels a new sense of responsibility, of purpose, and tries to pay attention to Mrs. Trilly. She's teaching them geometry, and this appeals to his visual sense of order and structure. Using a compass, with its deadly point, also is fun, and the day goes by quickly.

When he looks for his sister after the last bell, he finds her near the playground, with Frankie and one of his friends blocking her way. He can see them teasing her, and he walks quickly over there, hearing Frankie tell her that she's a chubby chink. He notices Lenny, and a brief look of fear passes across his face.

Lenny drops his book bag and breaks into a full-out run toward Frankie, who backs away, glancing at his friend, and then, when he realizes Lenny is coming straight for him, he turns and bolts.

Lenny tackles him at the waist, bringing him down and landing on top of him. Frankie cries out in fear, wheezing, until Lenny punches the back of his head, hammering down, and Frankie howls in pain. Lenny keeps punching and kneeing him in the back. He screams, and when one of the teacher's aides runs toward them, Lenny rolls off Frankie and stands up. Frankie sobs on the ground. The teacher grabs Lenny's neck, hard, squeezing, and says, "You're coming with me, you bully."

Mira yells, "It wasn't his fault!"

But the teacher yanks Lenny back to the school.

Lenny's mother has to close the store and pick both kids up, and the vice principal explains to her that fighting on school grounds is an offense that can result in suspension. Mira waits outside, and Umee says, "Both of them? What did Mira do?"

"No, just your son." But he explains that because it's Lenny's first offense, and the administration has had trouble with Frankie in the past, Lenny will be let go with a warn-

ing. "Another fight will mean an immediate two-day suspension."

Lenny watches his mother's expression, which is calm,
and she asks him what happened. Lenny tells her what he
told the teacher's aide and the vice principal, that Frankie
had been picking on Mira, and had bothered both of them
for weeks. Knowing that this will elicit a reaction, he says,
"He called Mira a chink."

His mother's cheeks redden and she asks the vice principal, "What will happen to the other boy?"

"I've already talked to his parents. Frankie has been suspended from school next week. It will be on his permanent
record."

"My daughter is upset. I have to take them home now."

"I apologize for taking you out of work, but the late bus
has already left."

She stands up and touches Lenny's shoulder. They walk
out, meeting Mira, who stands anxiously by the door, her
eyes wide and fearful, but their mother says everything is
fine. She then looks down at Lenny and says, "Good boy."

When she drives them home, she asks if this kind of
thing happens often. Lenny eventually tells her that it was
worse when they first moved here. He explains how he had
seen Ed fighting with someone from the neighborhood, he
and the other boy rolling on the cement sidewalk, grappling
and punching. The kids looking on taunted his brother with
cries of "chink" and "jap". Lenny was halfway down the
block, not sure if he should get closer, and when he heard
this he backed away.

"How come you never told me this?" she asks.

"Ed told me not to."

His mother grips the steering wheel. She shakes her head. After a while she tells them that tomorrow she is going to the doctor with their father.

Mira asks, "Can we come?"

"To the doctor? No. You stay home with your brothers."

She pulls up to the house. Before they climb out she tells them that she will eventually be much busier. "You two have to be good. I can't do this if I am working in an office."

"We didn't start it!" Mira says.

"I know, but you'll have to figure it out yourselves. What do you want for dinner tonight?"

Lenny and Mira say "McDonald's" in unison.

16

Lenny dials Nancy's number from the kitchen telephone, his hand shaking from nervousness. When the familiar voice answers he tells her who it is. She's quiet, and then says, "Oh, the collect call boy!"

"You gave me your number."

"I certainly did. It's funny, your calling me. How are you?"

"Okay. How are you?"

She laughs that whispery delicate laugh, and Lenny smiles.

"I'm good," she says. "I'm writing a paper for my psych class. Did I tell you I'm in college?"

"No," Lenny says.

Nancy is a junior at Hofstra University, and lives in one of the high-rise dorms near the highway, working nights as a waitress at an Italian restaurant. She tells Lenny she hopes to specialize in child psychology, which is why she accepted his collect call. "Any young kid who calls strangers like this has got be interesting. What's on your mind?"

Lenny doesn't know what to say, and after a few moments she asks, "Okay, tell me one interesting thing that happened to you today."

He tells her that he was almost been suspended from school.

"That *is* interesting. Why?"

When Lenny describes his fight with Frankie he finds it

easier to talk to someone he doesn't know. She asks about what Frankie said to Mira, and when Lenny tells her, she says, "Oh! You're Oriental?"

"Korean."

"Where are you calling from?"

"Merrick."

"I didn't know there were any Orientals in Merrick."

Lenny suddenly doesn't like her knowing too much about him, and he hangs up.

After practicing his kicks and punches in the back yard, he heads up to the train station but sees one of the neighborhood kids on a minibike, riding fast in the middle the street. They recognize each other, and the boy rides up onto the sidewalk to say hello. He introduces himself as Sal, short for Salerno, and asks Lenny if he wants a ride.

Sal is tall and lanky, with an underbite that seems to slur his words. He wears an AC/DC concert shirt and dirty jeans with holes on the knees. Long scratches cover his arms, as if he fell into a thorn bush, and his fingernails have grease under them.

The minibike looks like a lawnmower engine in a basic metal frame, the tires small and bald, and he controls the throttle with a shoelace tied to the springloaded switch on the engine. A thick cocoon of duct tape attaches the seat to the frame. Lenny asks him if he built this himself, and he replies, "Most of it. My dad helped. Get on."

Lenny climbs onto the back. Sal tells Lenny not to drag his feet, and they take off. There are no shock absorbers, so the ride is bumpy and erratic, and the shoelace throttle jerks them forward. Sal speeds down Wynsum Avenue, the engine whining, and Lenny grips the back of the seat tightly. Sal yells, "Hold on! I'm opening it up!"

He yanks on the shoelace and they lurch forward and speed about twenty miles an hour. Lenny starts laughing hysterically because he's scared, but he's also enjoying this, and when Sal brings them to a slow stop, using his sneakers as brakes, Lenny calms down. His hands hurt from holding the seat so hard. Sal shuts off the engine.

"Thanks," Lenny says.

"I saw your brother smoking weed last week."

"Yeah?"

"You go to school with my sister?

"No. I go to Birch."

"How come you go to Birch? We live right near each other."

"I'm on the dividing line."

"Too bad. You could've just walked across the highway to go to school. Take it easy. I gotta run." He climbs back onto his minibike, yanks the engine alive with the starter cord, and then slowly tugs on the shoelace, the bike drifting forward. He says, "Let me know if you ever need to buy some weed."

Lenny asks, "What?"

But Sal is already speeding away, his shirt flapping up his pale, bony back.

Because this weekend is Umee's doctor's appointment, the mood in the house is strangely subdued. Yul, although drinking as usual, is solicitous with her, cleaning up the McDonald's wrappers and washing the glasses in the sink. They talk quietly about closing the store, and Lenny hears them discuss other job options for her. They speak a mix of English and Korean, and his mother mentions her graduate work at Northeastern, and how that might help her get a secretarial job.

Umee's favorite novels are on the bookshelves in the basement, and until Lenny overhears her talking about graduate school he doesn't connect these novels with her schooling. He leafs through her paperback copies of Hawthorne, Twain, Faulkner and Steinbeck. In the margins are notes in Korean script, and when he brings *The Scarlet Letter* up to the kitchen he asks her what the notes are.

She skims them, smiling to herself. "Some words I needed translations of."

Lenny then understands that she read these in a second language.

She says, "That's one of my favorite novels. I must have read that twenty times over."

"Really?" he asks. The only books he ever rereads are his martial arts manuals. "Should I read it?"

"Try Mark Twain. Maybe Charles Dickens. Have you been going to the library?"

"For karate books."

"Oh, you should read fiction. It's more fun." She flips through the novel and says, "Books saved me."

"What do you mean?"

She smiles. "You'll see."

It's a quiet night for the first time in weeks, and Lenny keeps waiting for a fight to erupt, but it doesn't. Instead his parents go to sleep together in the bedroom, something that ends up disturbing him because it's so unusual. He hears them murmuring.

He has his mother's copy of *The Adventures of Huckleberry Finn* with him, and reads the first couple of chapters, studying the Korean notes in the margins. When he sees the brief note about the author in the back, he's amazed that this novel is almost a hundred years old and that his mother still likes it.

The house becomes quiet. He hears his brother in the kitchen, and walks out to see him. Ed wears sweat pants and a ratty T-shirt and eats a cold burger. He glances at Lenny and grunts.

Lenny tells him that Sal saw him smoking pot.

Ed smiles. "That dirtbag sells it. He's pissed that I didn't buy any from him. What are you doing hanging out with him?"

Lenny shrugs his shoulders.

"Watch out for him. He'll get you in trouble."

"Why?"

"Just watch out for him." Ed punches his arm lightly. "Who's going to look out for you when I go to college?"

"I can look out for myself."

Ed laughs. "Tough guy." He finishes his burger and goes downstairs. It occurs to Lenny that he barely knows his brother.

17

The lump in Umee's thyroid is a tumor, and she needs to go back in for more tests and a biopsy. She explains this to Lenny on the way to church. Mira stays at home with a cold, and Yul has work to do, something about looking for a new job. So Umee turns to Lenny, who sits in the passenger seat, and tells him that if the tumor is cancerous she might be in trouble.

"What kind of trouble?"

"It could spread. I need an operation no matter what, but they want to check the tumor first."

Lenny stares at her throat. Nothing looks different, but he imagines a pulsing tumor. She says, "I want to have your grandmother visit, to help out. She might come before my surgery."

"From Korea?"

"Yes. She will stay with us," she says uneasily.

He asks if Grandma ever visited before.

"Yes, when I was pregnant with you. She and your father don't get along."

"What happened?"

She sighs. "He told her to leave."

"He kicked her out?"

His mother says, "They are both very strong people. Very stubborn."

"What happened?"

"Your grandmother saw how your father treated me and

couldn't stand it."

"And she's coming back?"

"I need help. We have to close the store, and take care of you children. I need your help. You and Mira have to do more chores."

"Okay."

"And you have to pray for me."

Lenny doesn't know how to respond to this. He has never really prayed. Even when he was supposed to be praying at church he ended up looking around to see what everyone was doing. Although he understands the concept of God and prayer, he never really believed God could hear him.

His mother drives into the parking lot, and Lenny sees some of the other kids heading up to the children's service. He doesn't tell his mother about his plan to skip both the service and the Korean language lessons. He's here only for the tae kwon do.

They walk into the church, his mother patting his head and heading up to the main service while Lenny slows his pace, watching her, and then turns around as soon as she disappears into the chapel. He walks past other kids and their parents, and out to the small building by the cemetery.

There's no one inside, so he takes off his shoes and socks, and begins stretching out. He hears the music from the church carrying across the cemetery, and looks out the window. The voices of the choir swell and echo. The early afternoon sun lights up the tombstones—glistening black marble and polished white granite glaring back at him. He hears the congregation joining in, and the music fills the graveyard. Only then does Lenny fully absorb the fact that his mother might be sick.

The tae kwon do teacher singles him out again for his bad form, and humiliates him by making him stand in front of the entire class and practice a side kick a dozen times over. By the time the lesson is almost finished, Lenny's shirt is soaking in sweat, his thighs burning in his jeans, and he can sense all the other kids watching everything he does, waiting for him to mess up again.

The teacher has them do warm-down stretches, and finally, when they finish, Lenny runs out of the building and waits by the car. He knows his mother is having lunch with the rest of the congregation, but he doesn't want to go anywhere near the church. He promises himself that he will never ever come back here again.

He watches the other tae kwon do students file through the cemetery and back into the church, where they join their parents. Lenny sits on his car's front bumper, his damp T-shirt now cold. When his mother appears, looking for him, she sees his expression and asks what's wrong.

"I want to go home now."

"What happened?"

"I want to go home."

She studies him. "Did you get into a fight?"

"No. I just want to go home now."

"What about some lunch—"

"I want to go home!"

She sighs and touches his cheek. She says, "Do you know how important you are to me?"

Lenny looks up at her pale face, her forehead shiny. She gives him a sad smile. He says, "I don't like it here."

"All right, Lenny. Let's go home. Do you want to see a

movie?"

"Really?"

"Just us two."

She lets him into the car, and as they drive away he sees some of the other kids walking out into the parking lot eating sweet rice cakes, talking and joking with each other.

That afternoon Lenny torments his sniffling and coughing sister with the news that he saw *Meatballs*, and that she missed a great movie. Mira complains to their mother that it isn't fair, and his mother, annoyed, says that Lenny has to take Mira to *The Muppet Movie* when she feels better.

"But that's a little kid's movie!" Lenny says.

Mira gives him a satisfied "Ha!" and returns to bed.

Their father isn't home, and their mother lies down on the living room sofa and naps. Lenny gets on his bicycle and rides around the neighborhood, heading for the woods near the edge of town.

Cedar Swamp is a small creek fed by run-off and has streams that lead toward the canals of Newbridge Park and into the many tributaries that eventually empty into the ocean. Everyone calls it the "woods" or the "swamp," and in summer the neighborhood kids sometimes hang out there. Last summer someone strung a rope swing over the water, though no one went swimming—the creek often looks polluted, with strange foam, garbage, and rusted shopping carts piled near the large concrete drainage tunnels.

Large houses sit near the edge of the woods, leafy trees hanging over their roofs and shrouding them. Lenny studies them as he rides along the side streets, wondering what it would be like to have as your back yard this expanse.

There are wide, worn paths leading from the houses into the woods, and he locks his bike to a tree and walks deeper in, where the trees and shrubs grow dense, blocking out the traffic noises on nearby Sunrise Highway.

He comes across a wide, shallow stream and searches for turtles. Once he saw a small turtle swimming in the large creek, and although he didn't catch it, he couldn't stop thinking about it. He has been intrigued by turtles ever since watching a science show on TV about tortoises on the Galapagos that lived for hundreds of years. Then he and his sister watched a TV movie about an enormous sea turtle and its connection to a young couple. The couple found the turtle as a baby and drew a heart on its shell. The end of the movie revealed the same heart on the gigantic adult turtle. Both Mira and Lenny had been impressed by this.

Lenny doesn't find any turtles here, though, and continues walking along the stream. It's getting dark, and he knows better than to get lost in here at night, so he backtracks slowly, enjoying the quiet and solitude.

When he returns home he finds his mother on the telephone, speaking in loud and careful Korean. She says "Uhma" to the person on the other line, and he suspects it's his grandmother from the way his mother keeps repeating herself. He doesn't remember anything about halmonee, and hasn't met any of his relatives though he has a faint memory of his father's brother, Uncle Gil, a stooped, small man who ducked his head shyly. His mother told him that Gil and his father fought often and hardly kept in contact. Gil drives a truck for a grocery somewhere in New York.

His mother hangs up the phone. She turns to him, smiling. "Your *halmonee* will be coming next week."

"Here?"

"Your sister will have to sleep in your room. *Halmonee* will sleep in Mira's room."

"What?"

"Just for two weeks."

"Two weeks!"

"For me, Lenny. I need her here."

His mother rests her hand on his head. It's a familiar, comforting gesture that he remembers her doing ever since he was a baby. Less an attempt at soothing him, it's more of a way to connect them. After a moment he nods his head, and she pulls away. "Thank you," she says. "She speaks very little English, so you will have to try harder to learn Korean."

"I'm not going back to that church."

She sighs. "But you won't be able to talk to her."

"I'll learn it on my own."

She smiles. "How?"

"The library."

"Good for you. I am tired again. Will you find something for dinner? Make something for your sister too."

He heats up two cans of soup, toasts some bread, and calls Mira to the kitchen. Her nose is red, and her eyes watery, so he tells her that he'll bring her dinner to her room. "It's chicken noodle soup."

"When are we going to see the movie?"

"When you're healthy."

As he puts the bowl and plate on a platter, he hears his mother easing herself onto the living room sofa. He likes the peacefulness of the house with his father gone, and wonders what will happen with his grandmother here.

18

The Going Out of Business Sale at Sweets 'N Gifts is a failure. No one really wants to stock up on chocolates and rock candy. Some of the jewelry sells, but by the time the store officially closes, Yul and Umee have bags and bags of cheap silver earrings, necklaces, and even more bags of bulk candy. They have large glass display cases and shelving with nowhere to store it, so Yul wraps them in plastic and puts them in the back yard. Umee asks if there's any candy that the three kids want, but none of them do. Ed recommends they save it for Halloween. "Dump it then."

The last day of the store coincides with Umee's biopsy. She says closing the store keeps her mind busy, so she's glad to have many things to take care of. Her iron pills are helping her anemia, and she seems to have more energy. Yul drives her to the hospital while Ed, Lenny and Mira wait around the house, watching TV.

Mira asks what happens if the cancer is bad.

Lenny has no idea, and turns to his brother, who says, "If it spreads, she'll need chemotherapy."

"What's that?" Mira asks.

"Chemicals to kill the cancer, but it also kills healthy cells. That's why they lose their hair."

"Mom's going to lose her hair?" Mira asks, his voice rising.

"Only if it's spread," Lenny says.

"Is she going to die?"

Ed shrugs his shoulders.

Lenny says, "No."

"How do you know?" Mira asks.

"He doesn't," Ed says. "No one knows."

"God knows," Mira says.

"There is no God," Lenny says.

Both Ed and Mira turn to him. Mira says, "You're going to get in trouble for that."

"The Devil told me there's no God."

"Don't say that!" Mira cries.

Ed laughs. He tells them he's going out. Lenny asks him about Sal, if he really is a pot dealer.

Ed says, "Small time, but yeah. I'm telling you—watch out for him."

After he leaves, Lenny pulls out his marked deck of playing cards he ordered from a magician's catalog. He teaches his sister how to play Go Fish. The corners of every card has a tiny circular design similar to a clock, and Lenny can tell the card from the position of the dots. Lenny knows not only the next card in the deck, but most of the cards Mira has.

Because of the mail order catalogs for martial arts books and supplies, Lenny ends up on mailings lists for other catalog companies, and slowly he learns about the wealth of information out there. He has to buy money orders from the local post office, because he can't send cash, but other than that his age doesn't seem to matter. He recently ordered catalogs from a publisher of military manuals and espionage books.

He lets his sister win a few rounds, and then asks if she wants to bet money. She says she doesn't have much, and Lenny tells her they can use I.O.U.'s. He lets her win twenty-five dollars, and then asks if she wants to double the stakes. She does. Then he wins easily, and makes her sign an I.O.U. for fifty dollars. He tells her she has to pay him within a week.

"But I don't have it!"

"Well, I'll have to charge interest."

She looks mildly panicked, so he tells her he's kidding. He won because of his magic powers. She laughs it off, but he shows her how he can read her mind. All she has to do is think of the card she sees, and he can tell her what it is. After a few demonstrations she becomes suspicious. She studies the cards carefully. Then she says, "Hey, wait! Something is different about these."

He's surprised she notices the marks, and asks her what she sees.

"The dots are different. Are these...cheating cards?"

"It's called a 'marked deck'."

"Where did you get it? How does it work?"

He explains the clock code system and how he bought this from a mail-order catalog. She examines the cards again, and a gleam of amazement sparkles her eyes. She asks, "People actually make these?"

"They make all kinds of things."

"Like what?"

"Top secret. I can't tell you."

"You have to!"

Lenny leaves her throwing a tantrum. He walks out into the front yard and climbs the tall maple. He sits up on one of the highest branches, the telephone wires near his head. He rests there, wondering how his mother's biopsy is going.

Lenny jerks awake at the sound of Sal's minibike in the distance. He grabs a branch, startled that it's almost dark out.
Climbing down, he runs toward the sound of the bike, onto
Frankel Boulevard, and sees him racing up the street. He
waves him over.

"What's up, Lenny?" he lisps, his feet dragging the bike
to a stop.

"My brother said you're a small-time dealer."

He shrugs one shoulder. "I was. I'm expanding."

"How?"

"You don't want to know."

"I do. I won't tell anyone."

Sal stares at him for a while. "I don't think you would.
But the less you know, the better off you are."

"Do you make good money?" Lenny asks.

"Why?"

"I need to start saving for college."

He laughs. "Already? Shit."

"My mom said it can cost twenty thousand a year."

Sal nods his head slowly. After a moment, he asks, "How
are you with gardening?"

"I don't know."

"Do you like messing around in the dirt?"

Lenny looks down at his hands, which are dirty from
climbing the tree.

Sal says, "Okay, you want to see something?

Lenny says he does.

"It's secret. You tell anyone anything, and I'll make your
life hell."

"I can keep a secret."

"Hop on."

Lenny climbs onto the back of his bike, and Sal yanks the engine on. Lenny notices Sal attached a bicycle handbrake as a makeshift throttle—the tighter he squeezes the handbrake, the faster they go. Sal rides them to the woods, to the entrance along Sunrise Highway, and locks his minibike to the guardrail.

They walk down to the swamp and he leads Lenny around to the second swamp farther in. Then he says, "It's deep in. You ready?"

"Wait. What is it?"

"I might need some help."

"Do you have a flashlight?"

"Don't need one."

"It's okay," Lenny says, looking up at the dark sky. "I don't have to see it. I can't see anything anyway."

Sal replies, "All right. One reason why I wanted to show you is 'cause I'm looking for an assistant, someone I can trust."

"To do what?"

"Check on my plants," he says.

"What kind of plants?"

"What kind do you think?"

"Check on them how?"

"Make sure they stay hidden. If they're dry you water them from the nearby stream. I'd pay you."

"How much?"

He thinks about this. "You'd have to check on it once a day, like after school or something. Just until the crop is ready, so maybe another couple months, until mid summer. So... how about five bucks?"

"For all that work? Just five bucks?"

Sal tilts his head. "You would just check on it. That's easy work for five bucks a day."

"Five bucks a day?" Lenny says, shocked. He thought Sal had meant five dollars for the entire job. Lenny usually gets paid five dollars to rake a yard, maybe ten to shovel snow. He can't quite believe this, because it would be more money than he'd ever seen before. He quickly calculates thirty-five dollars a week.

"Think about it. Come by my house tomorrow and let me know. Thing is, it's secret. I mean really secret. You can't tell anyone—not your friends or your brother or anyone. I'd seriously fuck you up if you did. Can you keep a secret?"

"Yeah."

"I mean it, Lenny. This is serious shit."

"I know. I can keep a secret. I really can."

Sal studies him. "You know where I live? The house with the wooden shingles."

Lenny nods his head.

"Come by tomorrow after school." He looks down at Lenny's sneakers. "Do you have high tops or hiking boots?"

"Hiking boots," Lenny says.

"Wear those. And long pants. Let's go. I'll give you a ride back your house."

They trudge back to his minibike, and Sal speeds him home. Lenny has visions of the money he will be making, and completely forgets about his mother until he sees the Cadillac in the driveway.

Umee and Yul are annoyed that they won't get the test results for another two or three days. Lenny is fixated on the bandage over his mother's throat. She tells him that they used a needle to get samples from her thyroid, and the laboratory is now checking to see if there is any cancer. She will be getting an operation no matter what the results are, but the doctor wants a better idea of what the tumor is.

Lenny's father is already drinking. Lenny guesses that they were fighting in the car, because they move in separate orbits, ignoring each other, with none of the strange solicitousness he witnessed the other night.

Ed stomps through the back door, and their father yells at him to come to the living room. Lenny hears his father calling Ed a lazy bum. Ed is silent. The berating continues for a while, with their father listing all the things that are wrong with Ed, and finally Ed says, "I'm not the one who's probably going to lose his job because of incompetence."

It seems the entire house goes still. Lenny waits in his bedroom, and hears his mother getting out of her bed, listening. Lenny moves to his door and opens it a crack.

Ed yelps in pain, and both Lenny and his mother move into the hallway. She stops Lenny, and walks ahead. Ed runs outside. Lenny's mother yells at his father. When Lenny peers around the corner he sees his father's whiskey glass on the carpet, a large stain pooling near the coffee table. The strong odor of alcohol blows down the hall. Lenny sees his mother hold the bandage on her throat as she continues yelling, but she loses her voice.

Yul curses her in Korean, and in the barrage of deep-voiced yelling a few English words pop up: "deductible", "insurance." Lenny withdraws into his room, knowing what this fight is about—money, as usual. He looks out his window, which has a view of the backyard, and sees Ed pacing in his socks. Lenny realizes his brother left the house without his shoes, and doesn't want to come back in. Lenny opens his window and motions to Ed. This bedroom used to be Ed's, and there's a large closet with some of his old clothes and shoes in it.

Lenny searches his closet, grabs an old pair of sneakers and one of his torn jean jackets, and throws them out the window.

Ed says, "Thanks." He puts these on and disappears into the night.

19

After Sal floated the idea, Lenny spends hours thinking about the pay. Five dollars a day. Thirty-five dollars a week. Eight weeks of work: 280 dollars. An astounding amount. The most he ever earned was fifty-five dollars after a winter of shoveling sidewalks. Lenny can buy more books, more weapons, and even his own TV and VCR to watch kung-fu videos.

After school he cuts through a neighbor's side yard and heads to Sal's ranch house two blocks away on a street shaded with tall, leafy oak trees. Paint peels off the shutters and an old station wagon rusts in the driveway with blue tarp covering the back of it. A basketball and a pile of old, warped, wooden shingles lie stacked near the front entrance.

Lenny rings the doorbell.

Sal's sister Terry appears. Short with a blunt banged haircut, she looks at Lenny, puzzled. When he asks to see her brother, she calls over her shoulder, and Sal tells her to let him in.

Their house smells of wet dog, and Lenny then notices the sound of barking from the back yard. Cluttered with furniture, the hallway and living room are dark and shadowed, little sunlight coming in through the windows. Framed photographs—collages, weddings and birthdays—cover the walls. Terry points Lenny to a door at the end of the hall.

Lenny knocks.

The door opens and Sal puts on his jacket while walking out. He carries a backpack, says, "Ready?"

Lenny says he is.

Sal leads him out the back, where the minibike leans against the side of the garage. His dog, a young Doberman, barks and pulls against a long chain. Sal ignores it. He looks down at Lenny's oversized hiking boots and says, "Those look like clown boots."

"They were my brother's."

"Be careful on the bike. Don't drag your feet. You might fall off."

He starts the engine and climbs on, strapping his backpack to the handlebars, and waits for Lenny. As soon as Lenny settles down Sal races off, Lenny's boots stuttering on the ground.

Lenny wonders if he could buy a minibike with the money.

Sal brings them to the same spot as before, locking his bike up, and they hike down to the creek, jumping over a small mound of accumulated garbage pooling in an eddy, and down one of the paths. He says, "Always make sure no one is around. Don't be followed. No one knows about this, but you have to be careful. I'm going to show you the trail markers." He stops. "I mean it when I say you can't tell anyone. Not one person."

"I know."

He studies Lenny, then they continue deeper in, the path narrowing. Sal explains that this will be his first crop, so he's still figuring things out.

"Where'd you learn this?"

"A friend of a friend gave me a copy of a photocopied

handbook. Some guys wrote it a while ago, and it tells you basically what you need to know."

"Can I see it?"

"Maybe." He points to a tree by the path. "See the notches at the bottom?"

At the base are "x" marks etched with a knife. Sal points past the bushes and ferns, and moves through them, leaving the path. Lenny follows. They continue walking for another ten minutes, pushing their way through denser, overgrown plants and shrubs. Sal explains that because kids sometimes come here to drink and party, he planted the marijuana deep in the middle, where no one ever goes. He stops and motions to an oak tree with its large lower branches spread out like two arms. "This means we're getting close. After this tree look for the Birch tree with a 'v' with the bark all diseased."

Lenny points ahead. "I see it."

They climb through prickly bushes, and then Lenny sees past the Birch trees to a small open area, bushes surrounding it. They approach a narrow clearing about ten by twenty feet, with a dozen rows of young plants a foot and a half high. It's smaller than Lenny imagined, and Sal says, "It's my test crop. I'm still learning a lot. The light's not the best."

Lenny looks up. Large leafy oaks shade much of the area.

Sal adds, "Something about the soil is acidic, so I should've used lime, but they're doing okay."

"What do I do?"

Sal explains that he's worried about pests, that already he noticed something—maybe rabbits or rats—likes to chew on the young plants. He has already tried different kinds of repellents, but Lenny will need to check on the plants to make sure they aren't being eaten.

Sal says, "They're almost old enough to have a hard stem, but I'm still fighting the bugs off." He reaches into his back pack and pulls out plastic spray bottle. He hands it to Lenny. "Spray the plants. It's a special castor oil mix that rats don't like. I'll spread the blood."

"The what?"

He pulls out a plastic bag filled with rusty red powder. "Dried blood powder. It keeps the deer away."

"Where'd you get that?"

"Gardening store," he replies, and spreads the powder a few feet away from the plants, circling the area. Lenny sprays the plants with the oil, examining the small long leaves. Sal says, "I'm thinking of stringing up a trip wire to see if anyone or anything comes by at night. You'll need to check that."

"You check on this how much?"

"Every few days, definitely on the weekends. The next stage is figuring out the male and female plants and sepa-rating them."

"There are male and female plants?"

"I know. Weird, huh? You separate them because the fe-males make better and more smokeable weed. If they get pollinated, then the females start making seeds, and less of the stuff that gets you high."

"It sounds complicated."

"It gets worse. It's really hard to tell the males and fe-males apart until it's almost too late. It's giving me night-mares. This is a fucking full-time job."

Lenny laughs.

Sal smiles and asks, "What do you think? Can you do

it?"

"Five dollars a day?"

He hesitates. "The thing is, I can't pay you until I harvest it, dry it and sell it."

"How long will that be?"

"Summer. Late summer."

"Like August? That four months." Lenny calculates one hundred fifty dollars a month for four months. "Six hundred dollars?"

Sal shakes his head. "No, you wouldn't go every day after they get older. I'm just worried about right now. How about a total of three hundred dollars at the end? Cash. As soon as I start selling."

"You're going to make that much?"

"If it goes okay, yeah. These plants get big, and then I can probably get maybe six pounds, dried."

"How much do you sell it for?"

"By the ounce or gram?"

"How much for an ounce?"

"Two hundred dollars, give or take."

"How many ounces in a pound?"

"You don't know that? What the hell do you go to school for? Sixteen."

There are too many numbers to keep track of. Lenny tries to figure out sixteen ounces times six pounds.

Sal laughs. He says, "It depends on how I sell it. If I sell it by the gram, it's ten dollars per gram, a dime bag. That takes a while though. Some people want it by the ounce or more. If everything goes well, I can make three grand per pound."

Slowly it dawns on Lenny that three thousand dollars per pound with six pounds means Sal is talking about eigh-

teen thousand dollars. Sal sees the shock on Lenny's face
and adds, "That's only if everything goes well. Already I lost
a couple plants to the rabbits, and I don't know how many
will be the better-producing female plants yet. I'm hoping at
least half of that will work out. So, you don't have to worry
about you getting your three hundred dollars. Next time I'm
going much bigger. All right? Deal?"

Lenny replies quickly, "Deal."

They finish protecting his crop from pests, and Sal shows
Lenny the nearest water source, a small stream a few yards
away. Plastic milk containers are tied to a branch, and he
fills them in the stream. He says, "The soil is pretty moist
right now, but in the summer we'll need to do a lot of watering. I'll bring more of these soon."

He instructs Lenny to water the base of the plants, and
after they finish, he stands back and inspects the crop. He
says that if all goes well the plants could grow over eight
feet tall. The hardest part will be keeping everything hidden. Sal says, "You're going to feel the need to show off, to
tell other kids what you're doing. Don't."

"I won't."

"Make sure you're never followed. If you see other kids
around near the swamp, don't come here. Don't give anyone any idea that there might be something here."

"I won't."

"You understand how much is at stake, right? Not just
money, but getting arrested."

Although Lenny knows marijuana is illegal, he doesn't
make the connection to what Sal is doing until he says this.
Lenny asks him if he can be arrested for growing, not sell-

ing.

"Yeah. I'm a minor, so I'm not sure what that means, but we can get in a lot of trouble. Our parents, too."

Lenny hears the "we" and this sinks in.

Sal sees that this is having an effect, and says, "You get it, right? That's why no one else can know about this."

"I get it."

After he drops Lenny off he tells him that they'll go again tomorrow afternoon to the site. Lenny then walks to the Merrick Library to do some research. He tells the reference librarian that he's writing research report on illegal drugs and needs to find recent information. She directs him to the *Reader's Guide to Periodicals*, a thick green book in the reference section with listings of magazine articles. She shows him the list of magazines and newspapers they carry in the stacks and in storage, and how to request the magazines. She asks, "You're writing a report on drugs? What grade are you in?"

He tells her that he's in the advanced section, and it's extra credit.

Settling into a corner, Lenny discovers that the *Reader's Guide* gives him access to all kinds of information, and not just about drugs. He gets distracted when he sees an article about descrambling pay channels on cable TV. He doesn't have cable—he doesn't even have a TV—but he promptly jots down the issue of *Radio Electronics* magazine on the request slip, and gives it to the front desk. The librarian rings a bell, and a teenager appears. He brings the slip downstairs and within minutes reappears with the magazine, leaving it in tray. When Lenny leafs through the issue he finds schematic diagrams, plans, and instructions for how to build a cable TV descrambler from parts he can buy at any Radio Shack. He looks around, amazed.

Over the next three hours he learns about everything from how to tap phones to how to build an indoor green house. One article has a listing of "controversial" publishers and catalog companies, which he photocopies. He intends to send away for all the catalogs he can.

When he returns home, he's exhausted, and is surprised to find his parents in the living room, sharing a bottle of wine. His mother says, "The tests came back. The tumor is benign. I still need the operation, but I don't have cancer."

Lenny realizes that he had been trying not to worry about this, and when he hears this news he feels weak with relief. Maybe he's tired from all his research, but he suddenly needs to sit down. He reaches back for the ottoman and lowers himself slowly. His mother sees this, and she comes over to him, takes his head in her hands, and kisses him on his forehead.

PART III

Triplines

20

The days are marked by school holidays, weekends, and a countdown to Umee's operation. Lenny tries to impress his mother with his library research skills, and presents her with a few photocopied articles about thyroid surgery, including the statistics of how common thyroid nodules are, and how simple the procedure is. But his mother skims through the pages without really reading them, thanking him but saying that she doesn't want to know too much.

Lenny can't understand this, but lets it go. She may not like too much information, but he craves it, and armed with his research tools he sends away for mail order catalogs from a spectrum of small renegade publishers that specialize in everything from imported tae kwon do books to drug cultivation. And he continues his research at the library, where he begins running into the limitations of a small suburban public library—they don't carry any esoteric magazines— but he learns about magazine stores in Manhattan that carry many of the current issues. Manhattan is only a forty-minute train ride away.

The details of his grandmother's arrival are being worked out, and he can see this creating more friction between his parents. The tone of their arguments are subdued, though, as if his father understands the purpose of his mother-in-law's visit, and how she will be helping to care for the children and the house. The gist of the arguments are about the length of the stay, and Lenny hears them compromise on a two-week visit.

Meanwhile, the school year is ending, and although he doesn't share the excitement of leaving grade school and entering junior high, he does enjoy the prospect of the summer vacation. Over the next couple of weeks he finds school a major inconvenience, because tending to Sal's crops is much more time consuming that he had thought. The weather is warming and the soil is drying, so Lenny has to water the plants every day. Plus the battle against the pests continues, with some kind of flea beetle attracted to the young marijuana plants. Sal shows him the photocopied manual on growing cannabis, the images so blurred that they look like black smudges, and the section on pests recommends either a garlic spray or a limestone and wood ash mixture.

Lenny's mother has a jar filled with garlic cloves, so he spends an hour preparing the spray, shelling and mincing the garlic, and then blending it into a liquid. His fingertips reek of garlic, and his sister hears the blender wanders into the kitchen, wondering aloud what he's cooking.

"Nothing," he says.

She eyes him suspiciously.

He asks her where Mom is.

"Shopping. She wanted to buy more Korean food for when Grandma gets here."

"You know that I get the bed and you get the cot, right?" he says.

"I don't know why you can't share the basement with Ed."

"He's too old. When he leaves I'll get the basement."

Ed will be spending the summer in California with his friends before starting college, which means Lenny can take the room. He has already begun researching how to get free cable TV wired into the basement.

Mira watches him blend more garlic for another minute, and wanders back to her room.

He pours the pale clumpy garlic mixture into a jar, and cleans out the blender. Then he runs over to meet Sal who is fixing up the crawlspace under his house as a secret storage room. Lenny knocks on the small wooden door.

"Come in."

The small door swings up, and he sees Sal leafing through a porn magazine. Sal says, "You got the garlic spray?"

Lenny holds up the jar.

"All right. Let's go."

His mini bike is out of gas, so they have to walk to the swamp. Lenny recently learned that Sal had been left back a grade, and he probably has to go to summer school again. He barely goes to his classes, and can't even remember what courses he's taking. He says, "I don't care. They don't teach me anything I can't learn on my own."

"Like what?"

"I'm learning about genetics, like how to breed certain strains. I asked one of my bio teachers about dominant and recessive traits. He told me some stuff, but it only made sense when I had to think it through with buds and strains. I even got a booklet on how to produce female seeds with the strains I like. I can't ask my bio teacher about that. What's the point of school if I can do this myself?"

Lenny makes a mental note to look up books on genetics.

When they arrive at the site, they inspect the young plants, and find a few of the beetles chewing on the leaves. They try the garlic mixture in the sprayer, but the clumps clog up the pump, so they have to apply the garlic with their fingers, spreading it over the leaves. Sal says, "This smells like we can eat it."

The plants have already grown almost a foot since Lenny first started, and in just another couple of weeks, they will be hardy enough to fend off most pests. While pasting the leaves, Sal asks Lenny about his brother, wondering why he hangs out with the dirtbags.

"He does?"

"Just wondering."

Lenny says they aren't close. "I hardly see him."

By the time they finish it's getting dark, and Sal describes the motorcycle he's going to buy when he starts selling the crop. "It's a Kawasaki, so it's one of those jap import jobs," he says, glancing at Lenny, and hesitating. "Sorry."

"I don't care. I'm not Japanese."

"Anyway, you get more for the money. What about you? What will you buy?"

"Some books. A TV."

"You've been doing good work, so if everything turns out okay with the crop you'll get a bonus."

Lenny tells him that he has to go home now for dinner. Sal says, "We smell like garlic, man." He sniffs his fingers. "The things I do for my crops."

He smiles and punches Lenny lightly on his arm.

Sal seems lonely. Although Lenny occasionally sees him hanging out near the Gables movie theater on Merrick Road with a couple of other older kids, most of the time Lenny finds him either at his house or riding his minibike, and even when he sees Sal with his friends they seem more like people he just happened to run into. Maybe he's selling weed. Lenny wonders if that's why Sal asked for help, because he doesn't have anyone close to trust. Lenny knows that as a kid, he can be bossed and threatened, and ultimately discarded, although he begins to see that Sal has taken a brotherly interest in him. Once, while they tend his crops, he asks Lenny what he wants to be when he grows up. Lenny says he's thinking about being a martial arts instructor or a kung-fu star.

Sal stops checking the leaves. "Can you actually do that?"

"I guess so."

He looks impressed and continues working. Then he says, "What if you get hurt? Isn't that like a professional athlete?"

Lenny didn't think of that.

Sal says, "My uncle played college baseball on scholarship. He wanted to go pro. But he had shoulder injuries that made him lose his scholarship. He didn't have a back-up plan, so now he's working at a gas station."

Sal straightens up and pushes the hair out of his eyes. "You always need to have a back-up plan."

"What's your back-up plan?"

He points to the marijuana plants. "You're looking at it."

"What was your main plan?"

"To be a superhero."

Lenny laughs.

"Seriously. I was going to be a caped crusader. It didn't work out." He bends down and continues checking the leaves. "Besides, it paid shit."

By the time Lenny returns home his mother has prepared

Mira's room for Grandma. In a corner of his room sits a small green army cot his father bought at a surplus store. His mother tells him that he has to be a good roommate, because everyone in the family has to work together for her operation. Grandma will be arriving tomorrow. His mother's operation is in two days.

That night, while he gets used to the fact that he and his little sister are sharing a room—every time she moves on the cot it squeaks—he hears his parents arguing quietly. They move from the living room to the kitchen, where their voices are muted, shrouded by the humming of the refrigerator, and after a while it becomes quiet. His father listens to classical music. His mother comes into his room to check on them. Mira is already asleep.

His mother whispers, "I am so happy your grandmother is coming."

"I don't remember her."

"You were too young. But did I ever tell you how she raised four of us by herself?"

"A little."

She tells him that Grandma went to a high school founded by American missionaries, and they nicknamed her "Maria." She learned how to play the piano well enough to be hired at church services and weddings. She wanted to be a professional, but her father had forbidden it. But she encouraged her children to love music and literature.

"What did she end up doing to support you?"

"Everything. She was cheated out of a business deal for a lumber company because she was a woman, so after that she always ran her own businesses. She sold food to the Korean Army. She ran a small sneaker factory. She owned a coal mine. She ran a bus-driving business. She did whatever she had to. My father died from leukemia when I was very young, so it was up to my mother to provide."

"Do you remember your father?"

"Very little. Almost nothing. I was just a baby."

"What's Grandma going to do when she gets here?"

"Cook. Take care of the house. She will help me." She leans forward. "Be good and listen to your *halmonee*. And if anything happens to me…"

Lenny doesn't like hearing this.

His mother notices his expression and says, "Oh, everything will be fine." She kisses him on the forehead and tells him to go to sleep. She takes a deep, slow, unsteady breath, and he realizes that she is terrified.

21

Short and hunched, Grandma has thinning silver hair and wears a wrinkled beige pantsuit with large black shoes that clunk on the kitchen floor. She arrives late the next evening as they prepare for bed, and the presence of a stranger in the house—since they almost never have guests—throws everyone off balance. Grandma looks around the kitchen as Yul brings in her suitcase from the garage. Umee has on a big smile, her cheeks flushed, as she introduces her children to their halmonee. Grandma claps her gnarled hands together, taking them in, and asks Umee in Korean with an incredulous voice if Lenny is the same boy who used to be so small and skinny. Grandma holds her arms out for him. Lenny hugs her, and she speaks to him in Korean. She smells of mothballs and cigarette smoke, her wool jacket rough and scratchy. Umee explains to Grandma that Lenny can't understand Korean. They have a brief discussion about this, and then Grandma hugs Mira, saying her Korean name, "Won Hee," fondly.

Yul asks Lenny where his brother is, but Lenny doesn't know. They stand around awkwardly for a moment, until Yul picks up the suitcase and carries it out of the kitchen. Grandma says to Lenny, "Not see you since baby."

He nods his head. She looks nothing like his mother, and he finds it odd that this strange old woman is his mother's mother. Grandma pinches Mira's cheek and pats her head. Mira blinks and stares.

Yul returns to the kitchen and tells the children to go to bed.

Umee says, "Let them stay up. They should get to know their *halmonee*."

He shrugs his shoulders and retreats to the living room. Grandma watches him with a cold expression, and she says something to Umee in Korean, her voice low and hard, and Umee shushes her. They sit in the breakfast nook as Umee brings out leftovers and talks to Grandma in Korean while Lenny and Mira nibble on pajun, a seafood pancake, and dried cuttlefish. Umee speaks quickly and excitedly. Lenny hasn't heard her like this before, almost childish. Even her gestures are unusual—quick head movements and leaning forward over the table.

After a while Mira yawns loudly, making Grandma laugh. She pats Mira on the head again, and Umee shoos her off to bed. Yul comes into the kitchen and pours himself a whiskey on ice. Grandma and Umee stop talking.

Once Yul leaves, Grandma says something quietly, and Umee glances at Lenny, who pretends to be preoccupied with the dried cuttlefish, which is chewy and tough, and requires two hands to tear with his teeth. Grandma repeats herself, and Lenny knows it's something serious about his father from the way his mother tenses. Lenny is getting good at reading their body language, hearing the inflections, and he knows Grandma just told his mother she should leave his father.

They talk quietly for another few minutes, and then his mother waves the discussion away. She mentions the surgery tomorrow. With that Grandma stands up, pushing her chair back, and pulls Umee away from the table. Lenny's mother tells him to go to bed, and Grandma says, "Sleep good."

He watches them leave the kitchen, heading for Grandma's new bedroom, and when he sees that they have left all the food out, he begins putting it away.

In the morning Mira wakes Lenny up with her creaking army cot, and he needs a minute to figure out where he is. He hears his father arguing with his mother, and the smell of Korean food carries down the hall, an unusual smell for a weekday morning. When Lenny enters the kitchen he sees pots bubbling over and smoke rising from a frying pan. Grandma wears his mother's apron and mixes something in a bowl.

She waves him to the table. She pours him a bowl of *jook*, a rice porridge, and pats his head. Yul appears in the kitchen in his suit and tie, and looks around, shocked. He speaks to Grandma curtly, who replies in a scolding tone. His father throws up his hands and walks out the back door. The screen door slams shut by itself.

Grandma snorts to herself. Her annoyed expression fades when she glances at Lenny. She points, making an eating motion with her fingers. Mira complains that she just wants cold cereal—Frosted Flakes—but Grandma puts a bowl of *jook* in front of her, with a small container of soy sauce to add as flavor. When their mother appears, she sits down with them. Ed tries to sneak out of the back door, but she calls him over.

Grandma greats Ed warmly, and speaks to him in Korean. He understands most of this and nods his head. He sits at the table, and their mother says, "I go into surgery today."

They wait.

Grandma puts a bowl in front of their mother, who says in Korean that she can't eat before surgery.

"I've got to get to school," Ed says.

"Your father will be coming home from work early to drive me to the hospital, so I won't be here when you get back from school. I need you all to be good."

Ed, Mira and Lenny look at each other, and then they nod their heads to her.

Because the children can't really communicate with Grandma, she tries to connect with them through food, presenting them with platters that they like for the novelty but tire of quickly. She promptly stores these dishes in Tupperware in the freezer. She cleans constantly—scrubbing appliances, vacuuming, waxing furniture—and this is just her first full day. Lenny comes home from school and finds her on her hands and knees, scrubbing the kitchen floor with a rag. She pulls herself up and presents him with a snack: *kim bop*, rice and vegetables in a seaweed wrap. She tries to talk with him, but he can't understand her. She then pushes him out of the kitchen, pointing to the wet floors, and she goes back to cleaning.

When his mother returns home two days later, she has a long, inflamed, smiley-face scar over her throat that she immediately moisturizes with Vitamin E oil. She hugs her children tentatively, then goes to bed. The operation went smoothly, and the only real after-effect is her exhaustion.

Yul grunts a thanks for the dinner Grandma made, the stovetop sizzling non-stop while Umee was at the hospital. The smell of soy sauce and fried batter overwhelms the kitchen, and Yul leaves the windows in the kitchen open all night.

The tension between Yul and Grandma isn't obvious at first, because they are both focused on Umee, but as she recovers over the next few days, her energy returning, delighted at having her mother around, Yul becames curt. He complains about the constant smell and heat in the kitchen. He says that there just isn't room in the house for this many people. He then says that since Umee is feeling better, Grandma must go.

Lenny hears his parents argue quietly in the kitchen while Grandma watches TV with Mira. Everyone hears them clearly. Grandma sighs to herself. Umee raises her voice, saying in Korean something about the two weeks not being over yet, but Yul says she has recovered so there is no need for two weeks.

Mira tries to speak with Grandma, asking about what she did in Korea, but the language gap is too large. Grandma just smiles.

The fight in the kitchen grows louder, with Umee's voice scratchy and hoarse. Lenny glances at Grandma whose expression darkens as she sits tensely on the edge of the sofa. Mira is the only one watching TV, a variety show with a singer, and when Yul breaks a dish and yells something, Grandma stands up and walks quickly to the kitchen.

The voices stop. After a moment Grandma says something sharp, and Yul retorts back in a louder and more threatening tone. Grandma replies, and Umee tries to intervene.

Lenny tells his sister that they should go to their room.

She eyes the TV, weighing her options.

"Want to go back into the church?" Lenny asks.

She perks up, and they throw on their shoes and leave through the front door to avoid the fight.

Lenny and Mira enter the church through the back door again, and this time they go to the small auditorium where there's a stage and an open room that's used for a dining and meeting area. It's dark, but they find the light switch panel by the side door, and after searching behind the stage curtain they turn on one of the spotlights. Mira stands shyly on the stage. Lenny tells her to sing something.

"What should I sing?"

"How about that *Annie* song?"

Although they've never seen the musical, Mira received the record for her birthday, and learned a few of the songs. She steps forward and sings "Tomorrow." Lenny turns off all the lights except for the spotlight, and she squints. Her voice is quiet and nervous, so he yells for her to sing louder, and he moves toward the back, near the kitchen with two large serving windows. Slowly, as she realizes that she's essentially alone in the dark, she raises her voice and belts it out. Unlike Lenny, she has no speech impediment, and because of her constant mimicking, she has a good voice. She pretends to hold a microphone, making Lenny laugh. She raises an arm to the audience, giddy, and her eyes shine in the spotlight.

They return home and find their father sitting in his lounge chair, the coffee table turned upside down and the green ceramic lamp broken on the floor, the bulb lit and sending odd angles of light onto the wall. Broken dishes lay scattered throughout the kitchen. Their mother is crying in the bath-

room. Lenny and Mira walk by the bedrooms, expecting to
see Grandma sitting on the bed, but she's not there. He tells
Mira to play in their room.

"Where's—"

He puts his finger to his lips, shushing her. He walks past
the living room, avoiding his father's gaze, and checks the
basement. Ed isn't there, but neither is Grandma. When Lenny returns to the kitchen and looks out into the back, he sees
her sitting on the brick steps at the door, hunched over, her
arms folded tightly, and she stares down at the crab grass.
She wears only a thin sweater, and she's shivering.

Lenny opens the door, but then his father yells, "She
does not come into my house! This is my house!"

Grandma shakes her head at Lenny, waving her hand to
the door, motioning for him to close it. He does. She studies
him, her face wrinkling as she stares through the darkness.
She gives him a small smile and turns back around.

He hears his mother come out of the bathroom and yell
at his father. They continue fighting, and because Lenny
doesn't want to walk by them to get to the bedrooms, he
hurries downstairs and into the boiler room, the water heat-
er rumbling. He kicks his make-shift punching bag a few
times, the tightly-packed rags in the bag exhaling with each
hit. Farther in is the storage room, where old, moldy boxes
filled with clothes, books, photo albums and his mother's
old paintings have lain untouched since they first moved
here. Curious, he digs through the books, and finds stacks
of large art books—Leonardo da Vinci, Van Gogh, Monet—
with colorful prints.

He hears footsteps above thumping quickly across the
house.

More yelling, and then the back door opens. Grandma snaps at Yul, who bellows back, and when Umee screams, Lenny jumps. He hasn't heard her scream like that before. He runs to the stairs, unsure if he should go upstairs.

From down here Lenny can see the back door open, and after a minute of more yelling, his father pushes Grandma and Umee to the door. Umee tries to push back, but Yul easily knocks her aside, and shoves Grandma against the screen door. They argue, Umee crying, and she struggles with him. He hits her chest with an open hand that sends her flying back into the wall.

She lets out a strangled cry and collapses.

Everyone stops. Yul peers down at her. He sways drunkenly. Umee, curled up on the floor, holds her throat. Yul says something and walks back into the living room. Grandma kneels down and speaks softly to Umee who is sobbing, shaking her head, repeating something over and over. Grandma takes her head in her arms, cradling her. She coos, and Umee quiets down. Lenny returns to the storage room and leafs through the sketchings of da Vinci, whom his mother once told him was his namesake. His hands shake as he turns the pages, sweaty fingerprints staining the corners.

22

The first marijuana catalog arrives, simply a dozen pages stapled together, each page listing a book—or, rather pamphlets. But the pamphlets are all about growing and cultivating marijuana. The publisher, a commune in California, highlights their ten-year expertise with growing marijuana indoors, even in closets. Other titles include: preparing and cooking with marijuana, basic hydroponic gardening, lighting principles, and seed preparation. To order any of these, Lenny only needs to send a check or money order and they will send the pamphlets in a plain brown wrapper.

Although Lenny is eager to show this to Sal, his mother wants him to stay home with his sister because Ed has to drive Grandma to the airport. His mother says bitterly, "I am still recovering and he is sending her away."

Lenny doesn't know how to reply to this.

She says, "But I feel better. Stronger. Maybe my thyroid and my anemia kept me weak for many years."

Grandma appears in the living room with her suitcase. She wobbles toward him and opens her arms. Lenny hugs her, and she squeezes him tightly.

His mother calls to Mira, who also gets a hug.

Ed carries her suitcase to the car, and Grandma gives Mira and Lenny another hug, and says in a sad voice, "Good boy, good girl."

Umee takes her arm and leaves the house with her. Lenny watches them from the front window, and his mother cries briefly, then rests her head on Grandma's shoulder as they move slowly down the driveway.

After seeing Sal's crawl space Lenny wants a secret room. He tells Mira about Sal's hideout. "It's a long room with the ceiling only this high." He holds his hand to his stomach. He asks if she wants to join him exploring, and she does.

They begin in the basement, and find a small cubby in the main room that houses a water meter. His brother's room has built-in storage benches that contain more of their mother's books. Other than a sectioned-off area underneath the stairs, there isn't anything else of interest.

But when they check out the garage, Mira points to a small door at the ceiling. It's inaccessible without a ladder, so Lenny raises the ladder that sits on the ground, extending it up against the dirty concrete walls. As he climbs up, the ladder shakes, and he tells her to hold it steady.

The door, a piece of plywood painted brown, pushes in without any hinges. Lenny forces it open, dust and grit sprinkling down. He pushes the entire board aside and peers into the hot, empty space.

"What is it?" she asks.

"Attic. Is there a light switch down there?"

"I don't see one."

He climbs down, finds a flashlight in his father's toolbox, and hurries back up. Although he's initially disappointed to find a regular attic, empty, with shiny insulation strips layered all along the floor and angled roof, once he climbs up into it and walks along the narrow strips of wood, he knows that he's the first one up here in years. It's remote and removed from the rest of the house.

"I want to see!" Mira says.

He climbs down and hands her the flashlight. "Be careful. Watch out for demons."

She hesitates.

"And if the flashlight stops working, don't panic. It's dark but if you're careful you won't fall through the floor."

"Fall through the floor?"

"There's only one piece of wood to walk on. The rest is insulation."

"Never mind," she says, handing him back the flashlight.

He replaces the piece of wood, and lays the ladder back on the ground. He keeps thinking about the marijuana pamphlet that would teach him to grow a garden in a closet.

Sal is so excited and impressed with the mail order catalog that he hands Lenny fifty dollars in cash and tells him to order all the pamphlets. He doesn't want to do it himself because his parents open his mail. "After I almost got sent to juvie for stealing they don't trust anything I do."

"Stealing what?"

He laughs. "I used to work at a hardware store. I knew how to turn off their alarm. One night I broke in and stole a bunch of stuff."

"And they caught you?"

"Not right away. I got busted when I tried to sell a really nice drill. Anyway, I got probation and a fine. If I got anything in the mail, my parents would open it. How come your parents don't?"

Lenny says that he receives too many catalogs for them to care. He looks at the cash and says, "All the pamphlets will only be thirty-five dollars, not including shipping and handling."

"Use what you need and keep the rest. How long will it take?"

"Four to six weeks."

"That long?"

"Sometimes it's much shorter. I should be getting more catalogs like this one soon."

"Cool."

They're sitting in the crawlspace, and someone bangs on the ceiling. Sal sighs. "It's my mom. She's making me clean the yard. You have to take care of the crop today."

"Watering?"

"We got through the pest stage. They're okay for that now. Check how dry the soil is first before watering. And they're getting big. Noticeable. Set up trip wires or something to see if someone goes nearby." He gives Lenny a spool of thin-gauge copper wire. "Low to the ground, with a log or rocks tied it, so we'll know if someone other than us has been by. Make it so that you remember how it looks, in case they trip it and try to put it back."

"Why would they do that?"

"It's too early to harvest. If I came across someone's crop, I'd wait until it was close to harvest and then steal it."

Sal instructs him to set the wires ten feet from the plants, a perimeter tied onto a stack of rocks arranged so that he will know if they're tampered with.

The ceiling bangs again, louder and more insistent. "I gotta go," he says. "When will you order those books?"

"Tomorrow. I have to get a money order from the Post Office."

"Let me know. And show me other catalogs you get."

Lenny hops on his bicycle and heads to the woods.

After watering the plants, which are now his height, he sets up the trip wire, stringing it one foot off the ground, looping it around sticks he shoves into the ground, and tying it to a stick that keeps a small log propped up. If someone trips over the wire, the log will fall. He makes a mental note of where the stick presses up into the log—two inches from a knothole—and tests it a few times. It will withstand a small animal, but a person should easily trigger it.

He smells the marijuana leaves, which are beginning to have that sweet pot smell he recognizes. With summer approaching, the days are growing longer, and he realizes that he's missing dinner. He races back, and finds everyone at the kitchen table, including his father, who is drunk.

His father lectures Ed, who leaves for California the day after graduation, in only three weeks. Yul barely pauses as he glances at Lenny and says that the next time he's late for dinner he will miss it. Then Yul continues with his story about being a student in Florida during the mid 1950's, when there had still been segregation.

"I had to be better than everyone, black and white. Which b-bathroom could I go to? There was a black one and a white one. I couldn't use either!"

Ed stares down at his plate, his jaw tense. He holds his fork in his fist. Umee wears a scarf around her neck, and stares blankly ahead.

Yul continues, "I have to be b-better than my American coworkers because I am Korean. You have to better than everyone."

"If you're better, why are you about to get fired?" Ed

asks.

Their father hesitates, and then reaches forward to smack him, but Ed pulls away quickly. Yul then yells that Ed is worthless and stupid, and deserves to be a bum. Ed stands up and walks quickly out of the house.

Umee says in Korean something about how Ed is leaving soon and he should be nicer.

They argue. Lenny tunes out. Mira plays with her rice, drawing designs with her fork. Lenny plans his day tomorrow, including going to the Post Office during lunch period for the money order.

Then his mother says in English, "You are the one who is stupid. You pretend to be much more than you really are. It's sad."

Lenny and Mira look up. Both are startled, because to say that in English meant their mother wanted them to understand.

Yul promptly picks up his plate of rice and beef and dumps it on her.

She jumps back, yelping, and he throws his drink at her, the glass missing her and clunking against the wall and clattering to the floor. Bits of rice fall off her face and down the front of her blouse. She turns to the children, sauce dripping off her cheek, and tells them to go.

"You want them to hear this," he says. "You want them to see what a bad man I am? I will show them." He swipes everything on the table at her, the serving platters, the bowl of rice, the glasses—everything crashes around their mother, who backs into the wall.

Mira gulps air, about to cry.

Lenny grabs her arm and pulls her away. They hurry out

of the kitchen as their father says, "Do you want them to see this?" and they hear him hitting her. She cries out.

Mira's face scrunches up, and Lenny grabs her arm. "Don't cry," he tells her. "Don't."

She nods her head quickly but her lips tremble. Lenny is about to send her to her room, but something about the tenor of the fight in the kitchen worries him. Their mother fights back, yelling about how badly he had treated her mother. Lenny hears him punching or kicking the wall, the thudding almost shaking the entire house. He tells Mira to grab her jacket and shoes, and they leave through the front door.

"The church?" she asks.

He feels like climbing the maple tree, and tells her to follow him up. She says, "I don't know."

The hardest part is getting off the ground, so he gives her a boost to the first branch, and she struggles to climb it. She hugs the trunk. "I'm scared."

"Don't be. Just hold on." He climbs up after her, and settles in on the higher branch near her. They hear their parents fighting in the living room, then the bedroom, then the kitchen again. They track their parents' movements from the noise. When their parents move back to their bedroom, their voices fly out the window near the tree. Lenny hears his mother cry in pain, and she screams about wanting a divorce. His father laughs and says she has no job, no money, and there is no way he is going to support her. She will lose her children. She will lose everything.

This is all in Korean, and yet Lenny understands it.

Mira asks if they have to stay out here for long. "I'm getting cold."

"You should've brought a better jacket."

"You didn't say what kind."

"Just until it quiets down."

After thirty minutes, the stereo begins playing classical music. Lenny tells his sister that they can probably go in now. She says, "I can't get down."

He jumps to the ground and reaches up. "Come on. I'll help."

"I can't!"

"It's only like five feet."

"I can't! It's too far! I'm stuck!"

"I'll catch you."

"You won't!"

"I'll leave you here if you—"

"You better not! I'm calling Mom!"

"Wait, wait. Shh. I'll get a chair or something."

"The ladder! I want the ladder!"

Lenny hurries to the garage, and finds it difficult to lift and carry the large wooden ladder around the Cadillac. His sister calls out that he better not be leaving her there.

"I'm coming!" he yells.

Finally he manages to carry the ladder to the tree, and leans it up against a high branch. Mira can't reach it without letting go of the trunk, and says, "It's too far."

"You have to let go of the other hand."

"I can't."

He climbs up the ladder and reaches over to her. She clutches his hand and scrambles over him and to the ladder, hugging it. He laughs and tells her to climb down. As she does, their father opens the front door and demands to know what's going on.

"Nothing," Lenny says, jumping down. "We just wanted to see something."

"Put that back," he says.

"I am." Lenny carries the ladder to the garage, and his father appears in the doorway leading to the kitchen. He turns on the light and waits. Lenny has to lift the ladder up onto his shoulders again, and struggles with it.

His father says, "You are too weak."

This annoys Lenny, and he hoists the ladder higher, walking carefully around the Cadillac, but because he's off balance he trips and swings the end of the ladder hard against the car, making a thud. He loses his hold on it. The ladder bangs against the side of the car as it crashes to the ground. His father lets out a surprised bark.

Lenny stares at the ladder, thinking, Oh, no. His father hurries into the garage and looks at the car, running his hand over a deep dent.

"You stupid boy! Look what you did!"

"Sorry. It was too heavy."

"You will pay for this!"

"It was an accident!"

"You shouldn't be playing with the ladder. It's not a toy! You will pay for this!"

"I don't have the money."

"You will do yardwork," he says, pushing the metal around the dent. "Starting this weekend."

Lenny kicks the ladder and storms inside. His mother appears in the kitchen in a new blouse and her face clean, asking what happened, and he replies, "Ask him." He glances at the food and broken dishes and glasses on the floor, and goes to his room, hearing his mother beginning to argue with his father again, who yells something about how stupid the entire family is. The fight grows in volume as it moves around the house.

Lenny hears him chasing her down the hall. His mother opens his bedroom door and grabs him. She says, "Get your sister and go into the basement."

His father pushes her away, and she tells Lenny to go. She runs into the living room, his father going after her. Lenny opens his sister's bedroom door, and she's standing there in the center of the room, frozen. He tells her to follow him.

They hurry downstairs, and hear their father beating their mother, who sobs and begs for him to stop. The basement door opens—a flimsy folding door on rollers that squeak—and she tumbles down the stairs, crying out and grabbing the banister to stop her fall. The door closes. She struggles down the last few steps and sits on the floor, crying quietly.

Lenny and his sister remain still. Finally, after a few minutes, his mother looks up.

"Are you okay?" he asks.

She nods and pulls herself up. She limps to the old sofa, and sits down. She touches the side of her face gingerly and readjusts her scarf. She says, "We will sleep here tonight."

"On the sofa?" Mira asks.

"It'll be like camping." Their mother pats the cushions. "Sit."

They hear their father upstairs, talking to himself.

"Sleep here?" Mira asks.

"Just until later," their mother says. "Do you want to hear another folk tale?"

"No," Lenny says. "Tell us something real."

She smiles. "How about when we had to escape the Communists?"

"The who?" Mira asks.

"Chinese and North Koreans wanting to take over the country."

"How old were you?" Lenny asks.

"Mira's age. No, even younger. The Communists took my mother's house and everything in it. I was the youngest. I was too tired to walk, so someone carried me on his back. Many, many miles on his back. I remember breathing into his neck. But during one of the times everyone was running, the man carrying me was separated from my family and couldn't find them."

"What happened?" Mira asks.

"We were separated for two weeks. I thought they were dead. I thought I was all alone. But then we made it to Seoul, and my mother found me. I was so happy. After that we moved around every few months. It was hard because there were so many refugees and the war was going on. But I never left my mother's side after that. I didn't want to lose her again. And now I don't get to see my mother at all anymore."

They sit quietly until one by one they all fall asleep.

23

Umee has a large bruise on the side of her face that spreads over her cheek and up to her eye, and because of this she doesn't want to leave the house. She asks Lenny to buy a newspaper on his way home from school—she wants to start looking for jobs.

Lenny has so many things to do today that he barely pays attention in class. They're preparing for some kind of achievement test, but he can't concentrate on this. He just doesn't care. Instead he wonders which Post Office to go to—the one near the train station always gives him a money order, but he can go to the one near the school during lunch, and send off the order right there, since he has forms with him. He worries that the clerks at this new Post Office might think he's too young. He also worries about which newspaper to buy, and does it matter if it's a morning or afternoon edition? He worries about the trip line in the woods, hoping he set it correctly. He worries about the dent in the Cadillac and how much yardwork he'll have to do to pay it off. He has been grinding his teeth more every night.

During lunch he leaves the school and walks to the Post Office on Merrick Road, waiting in line with a few others on their lunch break—a man in a tie, women in blouses and skirts—and when it's his turn the woman behind the counter looks down at him with a smile. When he asks for a money order for forty-two dollars, the clerk says, "Of course, honey." She puts the order in a small machine and types in the numbers. The machine spits out the money order.

Lenny asks, "It doesn't matter how young I am?"

"As long as you have the cash, honey, you can have a money order. That's forty-two fifty, please."

He pays this, and fills out address forms, making sure the carbon duplicate is legible, then sends off the top copy with the order form. Every time he does this he's amazed at what kind of information he can find. He's expecting more martial arts catalogs any day.

At the nearby drugstore he finds two newspapers, *Newsday* and the *New York Post*, and also sees a copy of *Merrick Life*, which he buys too. He's already used up his lunch hour, and he hasn't even touched his sandwich. He takes a few bites while hurrying back to school, and feeds the crows.

He sees Frankie picking on a younger kid, another walker returning to school. Frankie pushes him off the sidewalk, and the kid stumbles onto the street. Lenny walks toward them, looking around to make sure no teacher's aide is nearby. Frankie sees him and backs away.

"Haven't you learned anything?" Lenny asks him. He puts down his back pack. The kid on the ground stops sniffling.

"Why do you pick on weaker kids? Why don't you pick on *me* now?" Lenny pushes him hard.

"You better leave me alone."

Impatient, Lenny does a quick roundhouse kick to his face, which connects solidly, Frankie's head snapping to the side. He falls to the ground, stunned. Lenny kicks him in the stomach and chest, and then gives him one final vicious kick in the face. Frankie howls as his nose bleeds. Frankie curls up tightly, protecting his body and face.

Lenny turns to the kid in the street, who stares at him in fear. "If he bothers you or anyone else again, let me know."

The kid nods his head quickly. Lenny turns back to Frankie. "You are so weak." He kicks him again, hitting Frankie's hands covering his face, and viciously stomps on his shoulder. Frankie yelps in pain, sobbing. Lenny finds that he wants to keep kicking him, but stops himself.

Lenny comes home to Ed packing for his summer trip to California. Ed has done something to his hair—it's curly and strangely glossy. Lenny asks him about it.

"Permed a little for the prom," Ed replies. He takes down his posters and boxes most of his belongings.

"You're going to the prom?" Lenny asks. "With who?"

"With Liz. Down the block."

"Is she your girlfriend?"

He snorts. "No. Just a friend."

"Do you have a girlfriend?"

He gives Lenny an incredulous look. "You think any girl wants to go out with an Oriental guy in this town?"

"Why not?"

"Because Bruce Lee never gets the girl. Chuck Norris does. Shit, even David Carradine is a white guy. You know? That show *Kung-fu*?"

"He's white?"

Ed laughs. "Oh, man. You're funny."

Lenny isn't joking, and is puzzled by this new information. Ed asks what Lenny is going to do with his new bedroom.

"I'm going to buy a TV and then I'm going to hook up illegal cable."

"How?"

"I think I need to hook it up to the wires up on the telephone pole."

"Be careful. Don't get electrocuted. And don't get caught. Dad will kill you."

"I won't get caught."

He points to Lenny's arms. "You need to work out. You're too scrawny." He flexes his large biceps. "You need to bulk up. I told you why I got strong, right?"

"Yeah. To fight Dad."

He says, "When I'm gone he's going to focus on you. You better be ready."

"I'm learning martial arts."

"It's more than what you know, Lenny. It's how you look. It's both. That's my advice to you. Get more muscle."

Sal and Lenny discover the trip wire has been triggered. The wire holding the stick and the log lies on the ground. Sal quizzes him on the construction of the trip wire, making sure it couldn't have fallen accidentally. He tells Lenny to set it up again, which he does, and Sal inspects it.

"Was it this solid?"

"Yeah. I checked it a few times."

"Goddammit. So someone came by last night?"

"An animal?"

Sal checks the plants, looking for leaves chewed on or the dirt dug up, but finds no signs of animals. He bites his upper lip, which exaggerates his underbite. He's growing a scraggly mustache, and his long, messy hair reaches his neck. He says, "Could be like a raccoon or something just looking around. Those things get pretty big."

"What do we do?"

"Water the plants, set up the trap again, and this time clean the area so that we can maybe see footprints."

Lenny examines the ground, but the leaves and hard dirt reveal nothing.

Sal says, "We just have to till the dirt, make it soft. Then we'll see if it's an animal or a person. I have a hand till at the house. I'll go back and get it. You water the crops and start clearing the leaves and grass."

Lenny begins working, remembering that his father is going to make him clean the yard this weekend for denting the car. The prospect of more gardening annoys him, but it will also give him a chance to inspect the yard for his own garden. Except for mowing the lawn, his father doesn't really care that much about the yard, and his mother, who used to have a small vegetable garden in the corner, no longer tends it. Lenny doubts either of them could recognize marijuana plants, especially if he scatters them throughout the bushes.

He clears the perimeter, and when Sal returns with a hand till and a small shovel, they begin turning over the dirt, smoothing it, and then reset the trip line, which they test a few times.

While doing this, Lenny tells him about ordering the pamphlets and about maybe trying to start his own garden.

Sal says, "If you do, I can totally sell it for you, with a commission."

"How much?"

"Fifty percent?"

"That's a lot."

"I guess. But otherwise you'd be taking business from

me."

"You can buy it off me."

He thinks about this. "We'll talk about it once we finish this crop. If all this gets stolen, then I just might quit trying to grow."

He inspects the trip wire one final time and says, "All right, buddy. Let's roll."

That night Lenny finds his mother at the kitchen table, reading through the help wanted sections and working on her resume on an old Remington manual typewriter that shakes the table every time she hits a key. The classifieds are neatly stacked next to her, torn from the paper and folded, and when he sits down next to her and looks at the ads, he sees that she circled various secretarial and office assistant jobs. She says, "There are many openings for office help. I think I can find something good."

Lenny reads her resume. Her last job was in Seoul, as a secretary at a mining company. She says, "That was right before I wanted to go to graduate school here."

"Where's Dad?"

"I don't know. He hasn't come back from work." She types a few letters, then says, "Someone said she saw him with another woman at a restaurant last week. Maybe he is having an affair." She continues typing.

Lenny keeps quiet.

After a moment she says, "I was stupid and scared to marry your father. I was in this country alone, and your father came along at the right moment."

She sighs and reorganizes the ads. "It was worth it because I have you and Mira."

She turns to him. "You were so sickly as a baby. The cleft palate, the allergies, the crying. All I prayed was for you to be healthy. And look at you now."

"I still have allergies."

"Nothing like when you were a baby. And the cleft palate! Even after the surgeon fixed your uvula, you couldn't swallow anything without it coming through your nose. So you were becoming malnourished. You'd drink milk and it would all spill out. I had to feed you only a little at a time. A sip at a time. It took hours. You had to learn how to drink."

Lenny doesn't tell her that sometimes if he drinks too fast he still spills liquid out of his nose.

She yawns. He notices the bruise on her cheek is yellowing around the edges. She kisses his forehead and tells him to go to bed. As he leaves the kitchen she asks, "Just to make sure: If your father and I split up, you'd want to live with me, right?"

He turns to her, incredulous. "Yes. No way I'd want to live with him."

She smiles sadly and goes back to the typing. He hears the heavy intermittent clacks as he walks down the darkened hallway to his bedroom.

24

Sal and Lenny discover not only the trip lines triggered again, but they find scuffmarks in the dirt that could be footprints. But they aren't sure. Sal curses, and says, "Maybe it was someone covering up footprints."

The scuff marks move along the edge of the crops and then circle back. Lenny says, "Could've been an animal."

"Maybe. But it looks like whoever or whatever was inspecting it. And what kind of animal leaves this kind of trail? Where are the footprints?"

"A beaver dragging his tail."

Sal laughs. "When was the last time you saw a beaver here?"

"Never know."

He stares at the ground, scratching his scraggly goatee. "If it's a person I'm screwed."

"What are you going to do?"

"It's way too early to harvest. Haven't even started pruning yet. Crap. I'm going to have to ask Tommy what to do."

"Tommy?"

"A friend who used to do this. He's the one who sold me the seeds, and gave me the manual. I might have to stay out here and find out who or what it is."

"Sleep out here, you mean."

"Yeah. Catch him. Then scare him away."

"How?"

Sal shakes his head. The weight of this seems to sag his

shoulders, hunching them, and he motions to the stream ahead and says, "Let's water them."

They fill the plastic milk jugs from the stream and water the rows of plant, now fully at Lenny's height. They're quiet at first, as they focus on the job, and Lenny likes the peacefulness of the woods, the only sounds the nearby stream and birds chirping above. Then, after they finish, Sal inspects the plants and he gives Lenny an impromptu lesson. He points to the tops, telling him that he will soon clip them to increase the new shoots below. This also prevents the plants from getting too tall. He explains the procedure of sexing the plants—figuring out which ones will be male and female—by waiting until they begin to flower: male plants have pollen-bearing flowers, and the female plants have seed-bearing flowers. "Then you harvest the males because you don't want them to spread their pollen. The females make stronger weed that way."

"You don't smoke the males?"

"Oh yeah, you do. They're pretty strong right before they flower. It's all about timing, which is why this fucking guy is making everything harder." He kicks the dirt.

"Without pollen, you won't get seeds, though."

"No need. You can buy seeds easily. I still have seeds for this crop. You can store them for a while in airtight jars as long as it's cool and dry. I have a huge jar in the crawlspace."

"Can I buy some?"

"Hell, if this is someone going to rip me off, I'm probably out of business. I'll give you the seeds." He sighs and continues inspecting the plants. He says, "I'm not sure what the point of all this is anyway."

"What do you mean?"

"I grow it, sell it, and then what? Do it all over again? What's the point? I'm thinking I need to figure out what I really want to be doing."

"For a job?"

"For everything. You know? I need to figure out my life, man."

Lenny thinks about this as he watches the trees swaying in the breeze.

A new catalog arrives, a publisher of old military manuals from around the world, including fighting techniques of British commandos and books about Ninja techniques, written by former Ninjas. Lenny spends hours studying the catalog, trying to decide what he wants to order. The listing for *Secret Techniques of the Ninja* is the one that he keeps turning back to, and marks this as his first purchase with the money he'll make from Sal.

His father calls him into the living room. Lenny finds him in his usual spot, a tall glass of whiskey with ice sitting on the armrest. He says it's time for Lenny to work on the yard: rake the front and back yard for any leaves and sweep the sidewalks. Tomorrow morning, Saturday, Lenny will mow the lawns and trim the hedges.

"Now?" Lenny asks. It's getting dark.

"Now?" his father mimics, his lip curling. Lenny gauges that he has had four drinks, maybe five—it's almost at the turning point, when Lenny has to disappear.

"Yes, now," his father says. "The d-dent will cost two hundred dollars to fix."

Lenny knows that arguing won't make a difference, so he puts on his sneakers, and grabs the rake from the garage.

He moves across the lawn haphazardly, gathering up the few leaves and the many maple keys that cover the lawn. He piles this on the sidewalk, and searches for the broom.

In the garage he looks up at the attic doorway, wanting to use that space for something, but he isn't sure what.

His father appears from the kitchen door. "Why aren't you working?"

"I'm looking for the broom."

He walks down past the car, staring at the dent, and comes outside. He looks at the lawn and says, "Sloppy. There are leaves under the b-bushes."

"You didn't say rake the bushes."

His father turns to Lenny. "Are you g-getting stupid? I told you to rake all the leaves. There are leaves under the b-bushes."

Lenny picks up the rake and stabs beneath the bushes, the metal prongs snagging and bending back. His father watches for a moment. He looks down at the sidewalks and says, "You shouldn't put everything here. You should b-bag the leaves on the lawn."

Lenny doesn't reply, growing angrier. The leaves under the bushes are stuck in there. He has to reach down and yank them out by hand. He turns to see his father kicking the mounds of leaves and seeds across the sidewalk.

"What are you doing?" Lenny yells.

His father sways as he says, "I'm showing you why you shouldn't p-pile it on the sidewalk."

"But I just raked that!"

"Rake it again."

Lenny throws down the rake. "That's not fair."

"Fair? Life isn't fair. P-Pick up the rake and finish the

job."

"If you're going to mess it up again, why should I?"

He says in a low voice, "Because I told you to."

Lenny wants to defy him, but considering how many drinks his father has had, it's risky. He remembers what Ed said, that he would be the new target. This is what he has to look forward to. He picks up the rake and continues working, his father hovering. He says, "You need more d-discipline. You are becoming like your b-brother. Lazy. Soft. When I was your age I had to get up b-before dawn to do chores. Your mother b-babies you. She always has. How do you expect to get anywhere in this world by b-being lazy?"

Remembering Ed's comment about why he worked out, to be stronger than their father, Lenny knows his father wouldn't talk to him like this if he wasn't a kid.

Lenny smolders and thinks, You just wait.

His father stares off into nothing, a glazed look in his eyes. His potbelly hangs over his belt, his body settling. Lenny wonders, This man used to kill people?

By the time Lenny finishes the raking and sweeping, it's dark and his father has long since returned inside. Exhausted, his hands sore and aching, his nose running from his hay fever, he limps inside. His father has fallen asleep in his lounge chair and his mother has gone to bible study. Mira has found the typewriter their mother left on the kitchen table and is working on her new book.

Lenny peers over her shoulder, but she covers up the paper. "It's not ready," she says.

"What is it?"

"It's a novel about the animals who live in the church."

"The church across the street?"

She nods her head.

"What kind of animals?"

"All kinds. Mostly mice and bats."

"Bats. In the tower?"

"Oh. I didn't think of that. These ones live in the rafters."

It occurs to him that there must be a way up to the bell tower. There are no real bells, but a loud recording of them that the church plays on special occasions, usually weddings and Easter Sunday, but once Lenny saw someone up there cleaning. "Next time we'll explore it," he says.

"And can I sing again?"

"Yeah. Pick a better song, though."

The next morning Lenny wakes up, startled to see his father standing over him. After a minute his father walks briskly to the window, and opens it, saying, "Get up. Time to work on the yard."

Lenny looks at the clock. Six a.m.

"Now?"

As his father passes his bed he pulls the sheet off and throws it on the floor. He leaves the room and opens all the windows in the house, the shuddering and squeaking runners unused during the winter. The morning chill seeps into Lenny's room as he dresses, shivering.

Outside, he's glad to be moving and exercising. He finds an old pair of hedge trimmers that look like large scissors, and clips away at the overgrown bushes along the side of the house, using this as way to strengthen his arms. He considers this a part of his martial arts training. He also looks for plots of land to grow marijuana, and finds at least fifteen square feet in the back, next to the house, hidden by large leafy bushes. Lenny may be able to use his mother's old garden, but will have to be careful, since it's in view of the kitchen window.

Hard-packed dirt surrounds the back of the house, and he'll have to do plenty of prep work for it. He considers telling his parents that he'll take over all the yard work, and then slowly change some of the bushes to shield his crops.

His father, who has changed into a sweat suit, wheels out the lawn mower and leaves it in the driveway. He stretches his legs and arms for a few minutes. Lenny then watches with surprise when his father jogs down the street and turns the corner.

The lawn mower doesn't start. Lenny yanks the starter cord a dozen times, but the engine refuses to turn over. He checks the gas. The tank is full. Finally he has to wake his brother up. Grumbling, Ed checks the same things, and with one quick pull, gets the engine going. It sputters loudly. He kills it.

He rubs the sleep from his eyes and says, "I'm telling you. You need more muscle. Where's Dad?"

"Jogging."

Ed looks puzzled, unsure if Lenny is joking.

"No, really."

Ed laughs.

"He looked funny," Lenny says.

"I bet. Humpty Dumpty in Pro-Keds." He surveys the yard. "Now you're going to have to do this? Man, I feel sorry for you. I once forgot to weed the lawn, and like a thousand dandelions came up almost overnight. He was so mad that he made me come out here with a flashlight and pull each one. It was a school night. I didn't finish until like three in the morning." He sighs. "I am so glad to be getting the hell out of here."

He points to the lawn mower. "You try. Brace yourself with your feet, one foot on the engine. Pull with both hands in line with the cord. Not up or to the side, straight out." He opens the throttle and motions to the mower.

Lenny follows his directions and yanks the cord, and the engine sputters, but then Ed opens the throttle even more, and the engine catches, roaring. Ed nods to him and walks sleepily back into the house.

25

Lenny sees this time as the beginning of the end of his parents' marriage. A confluence of factors, including his mother's surgery, Grandma's truncated visit, Ed's leaving for California, and, most important, her finding a job, all push her to leave his father. And this only heightens the tension between them.

The job comes easily. His mother applies for a slew of secretarial positions, and one of her first interviews is with a real estate broker, who hires her on the spot. She comes home after the interview, flushed, excited, and tells Lenny that she begins her new career on Monday. "I want to celebrate," she says. "Do you want to get ice cream? Where's Mira?"

"Out with her friend Stacy."

Friendly's restaurant is in Bellmore, less than a mile away from her old candy store, and they sit in a booth near the front; his mother eats a small bowl of ice cream while Lenny has a junior sundae. She explains her job—secretary and office manager—and says with excitement that her boss suggested that she study for the Real Estate Broker exam, taking night classes, because eventually he will be expanding.

"He said my speaking Korean will help expand the business. It's a new career for me."

Lenny nods his head, beginning to feel ill from too much ice cream. "Is Dad getting a new job?"

"He's trying. He thinks he deserves a bigger job, a higher position, but no one else thinks that."

"He's drinking more."

She doesn't reply.

"He's making me do all the yardwork."

"I know."

"Why is he like this?"

She says, "He used to be worse. Do you know that while I was pregnant with you we had a fight and he kept kicking me in the stomach?"

"With me there?"

"Yes. I was so scared for you. And when you were born with the cleft palate and so sickly, I always wondered."

Lenny makes a mental note to research this at the library. "Was I okay?"

"Yes, but I was so mad that I grabbed a knife and went after him."

"Really?"

"He locked himself in the bedroom. This was in New York. I stabbed the door at least a hundred times. I went crazy. I didn't know what I was doing."

Lenny has trouble imagining this. "Then what happened?"

"I broke the knife. But there were many, many marks in the door that reminded me of how crazy I was. I think it also scared your father."

They fall quiet. Lenny can't eat any more ice cream.

His mother asks how Mira likes band, which she recently joined.

"I guess okay. I don't understand why she chose the viola."

"She likes to be different."

"I've never even heard of the viola."

"Let's buy Mira something for when she comes home. What would she like?"

He's surprised that his mother doesn't know. He says, "Chocolate ice cream is her favorite."

When they return home he climbs up the maple tree and stays hidden when his father drives up in his Cadillac and calls out to him, no doubt wanting him to do more yard work. Lenny stays quiet, thankful that the large, green maple leaves have grown in and shield him. His father has loosened his tie and rolled up his sleeves. He looks tired. He trudges into the house and calls for Lenny again.

Sal rides up on his minibike, and Lenny quickly climbs down and meets him on the street. He tells Lenny that he tried to sleep out with the crops last night, but couldn't stay awake. "I need to do this with someone in shifts."

"Did anyone come?"

"No footprints, and the trip wire was fine, but maybe that was because he saw me. And it got cold. Can you tell your parents that you're sleeping over my place?"

"Yeah. I'll call you later."

He says, "Thanks, buddy. You'll totally get more money for this. This is a lot to ask, I know."

Lenny's father opens the front door, calling him. Sal rides away, and Lenny walks back to the house.

His father asks who that was.

"A friend. I'm going to sleep over at his house tonight."

"No."

Lenny looks at him, puzzled. He has never cared what

Lenny did with friends. "What?"

"You can't be friends with *b-bob-tong* like that."

"A what?"

"*Bob-tong*. Dumb." He juts out his lower jaw, imitating Sal's underbite. "He is also low class. You should be friends with high class people."

"Sal's not dumb."

"You get different friends."

"You don't tell Ed who he can be friends with."

"And look at him. You can't go."

"You can't tell me what to do," Lenny says.

"I am your father. I can make you do anything. You finish raking the leaves now."

Lenny is so sick of him that he says, "If you want the leaves raked, do it yourself."

His father jumps down the steps so quickly that Lenny isn't sure what's happening. When Lenny realizes that his father, still in his socks, is heading for him, he turns to run, but he's too slow. His father backhands him across the face, spinning him, and he staggers back and falls to the ground. His eyes blur, a dizziness swooning him.

His father says, "Never talk back to me like that again."

It has been almost a year since he last hit Lenny like this, and that time had been more of a hard swat on the arm, punishing him for spilling his juice all over the rug. That stung, but this feels like he had rattled loose Lenny's brain, and he's too stunned to cry.

"Do you understand me!" his father yells.

His mother then appears in the doorway and cries out something in Korean. When his father turns to her to tell her to shut up, Lenny gets up and runs.

Lenny waits for Sal at the crawlspace door, and when he
hears the minibike he walks out from the side of his house.
Sal seems puzzled, and says it's too early to camp out.

As he approaches he peers at Lenny's face. He hesitates,
as if trying to decide to ask about it, but says, "My mom lets
me bring my dinner down here. Want anything?"

Lenny is still full of ice cream and shakes his head. Sal
unlocks the door to the crawlspace and tells him to wait
here.

He returns with a plate of meatloaf and greenbeans, and
they sit hunched over while Sal eats and Lenny leafs through
one of his porn magazines. Lenny asks how Sal got these.

"Stole them. You slip it under your shirt while you buy
a comic book or something. It's real easy. You can have that
one if you want. I'm sick of it."

"Thanks."

"You don't have a sleeping bag or anything?"

"I didn't have time to get it."

"Can you sneak back to get it later?"

"Probably."

"All right. We'll wait until it gets dark, and then head
out." He finishes his meatloaf and throws his green beans
outside. He says, "Your dad do that?" He motions to Lenny's face.

Lenny keeps looking at the magazine.

"Tommy's father is like that. When he was younger his
dad used to take a belt to his bare back to the point of bleed-
ing. He once showed me the crazy marks. He's got scars
now."

"Does his father still do that?"

"Tommy left home a couple years ago. He lives with his brother in Freeport."

Sal turns on a mini black and white TV, and he watches a game show while Lenny continues reading. He finds an issue of *Penthouse*, and likes the letters. He becomes so engrossed that he's surprised to see Sal preparing to leave—it's dark out.

Sal packs a sleeping bag and some gear into a duffel bag, and they walk to Lenny's house where he sees the lights on in the kitchen. He tells Sal to wait in the back yard while he walks in through the back door. He finds broken plates and glasses strewn throughout the kitchen. He hears his father mumbling to himself in the living room. Luckily his sleeping bag is stored in the basement, so he doesn't have to walk by the living room. He creeps downstairs, grabs the bag, and goes into the garage to get a flashlight. He's about to sneak back outside when his mother appears in the kitchen, asking where he's been.

He tells her he's sleeping over Sal's.

She sees his face and she bites her lip. She says, "I told your father that I am divorcing him."

This makes him pause. "Okay."

"He was very mad."

Lenny nods his head.

"I met Sal's mother. She is an artist."

"I didn't know that."

They're quiet for a moment, then his mother says, "Don't stay up too late."

"Okay."

"I will see you in the morning."

"Okay."

"You know how much I love you, right?"

"I know."

Lenny walks out the back door. As he and Sal leave the yard, he sees his mother watching them from the kitchen window. She looks so alone and sad.

Sal and Lenny's steps are out of sync—Sal has long shuffling strides and Lenny hurries to catch up. Lenny asks what they're going to do if they catch someone.

He says, "Scare him."

"How?"

He pulls out a handgun from his bag.

"Is that real?"

"It's a BB-gun. It can't really do more than sting, but it looks good."

"Can I see it?"

He hands it to Lenny, the gun heavy and too large for his fingers.

Sal says, "You can't do anything but have target practice. You can barely even kill a squirrel with it." He takes it and shoots a garbage can. Lenny expects to hear an explosion, but it's only a small click and the *ping* of the metal garbage can.

Once they reach the woods, Sal pulls out a flashlight. Lenny turns his on. Everything looks different at night. The trees and bushes crowd them, their flashlights hitting the branches and casting shadows around them.

Sal says, "It's so quiet."

"I can't even tell which is the right way."

"I know. I almost got lost last night. Just keep looking for the trail marks."

Lenny follows Sal as he leads them through the woods and to the crops. He shines his light down onto the trip wires, which are undisturbed, and along the smooth dirt. "Looks good," he says. "I was thinking we'd sleep over there." He points his light to the bushes. "I cleared an area behind them."

They kick clean the area again, and lay out their sleeping bags.

"I can take the first shift," Sal says.

"I'm awake."

"All right. You take the first shift. Wake me up in like two hours. Here's the gun. If you hear anyone, wake me up."

Sal curls up in his bag and falls asleep almost immediately. Lenny sits up, wrapping the sleeping bag around his shoulders, and listens to the crickets and the faint water sounds from the nearby stream. His cheek and temple still hurt from his father's backhand, and he hopes for a huge bruise so his father will see it.

As he sits quietly in the woods in the middle of the night, Sal sleeping deeply, he closes his eyes and practices meditation. Some of the Kung-fu books discussed breathing techniques and how to use the flow of chi through your body, but he usually skipped those parts for the cool kicks and hand techniques, but now now he wonders if he should learn more about chi and breathing.

There's a rustling in the nearby brush, and he opens his eyes. It sounds like a small animal. Lenny raises the gun, aims the flashlight toward the sound, and stands up slowly. The flashlight beam hits a small raccoon. It freezes, its eyes reflecting the light and blinking back at him. He aims the gun and fires. The BB pellet hits the hind leg, and the raccoon jumps, letting out a startled cry, and then scurries away. Lenny sits back down, his heart beating loudly in his ears.

He closes his eyes and tries to meditate.

26

Although Lenny is exhausted, he likes being outside. But the lack of sleep and the cold have worn him down and he's beginning to feel sick. Sal and he didn't hear anyone in the woods and they walk home in the morning, shivering and aching. Sal confesses that he doesn't think he can keep doing this. He says, "This is just too fucking hard."

The next day Lenny gets the flu. He spends two days in bed, feverish and coughing, reading about meditation. One story appeals to him, about a Shaolin monk who achieved such a deep state of meditation that he learned how to slow down his body functions, including his heart rate and breathing. He lived to be one hundred and ten years old. Lenny decides to practice this as well.

Elementary school graduation is approaching, just a simple ceremony in the main auditorium, but he doesn't tell his parents about it. Even though they both want him to do well in school, they hardly know what's going on. His mother checks his report cards before she signs them, but since he receives all E's and V's—"Excellent" and "Very Good"—she doesn't ask him about it.

By the end of the week he recovers, but pretends to be sick in order to miss more school. His mother, busy with her new job, barely has time to prepare meals or clean the house, let alone worry about what homework assignments Lenny is neglecting. She and his father fight a couple more nights, but toward the end of the week they must have resolved something because an uneasy silence floats between them. His father drinks more, but broods quietly, and seems to have forgotten his vigilance with the yard work.

The first day back to school Lenny finds himself taking a standardized test. It's a strange day. They are in the final week of classes, with their graduation next week, and after their usual current events session during which two students present an article to discuss, Mrs. Trilly hands out a booklet and Scantron forms. Lenny, so unused to sitting in a classroom, and definitely not ready for a test, barely pays attention to the instructions. They have to use number two pencils, mark their answers on the forms, and they have until the lunch recess bell to answer as many questions as they can.

When the tests begin, he notices that some of the other kids seem nervous. He shrugs this off and looks through the questions. Some are math-related, some are reading comprehension, others are puzzle and visual problems. They all seem stupid to Lenny, but he answers them without much effort. Some of the questions are strange, involving which shapes "fit" with which groups, or which lines and circles come next in a series. He doesn't understand why he's wasting his time with this.

After forty minutes, one of the students finishes early. Mrs. Trilly collects her booklet and answer sheet, and tells her she may go outside for recess early. The girl, Christina, smiles smugly at the rest of them, and heads out to the playground by their window. Some of the other kids work faster. Lenny watches Christina bouncing a red kickball by herself, waiting for them. A few others finish early, and they quickly hand their booklets and forms in, and run out.

Now everyone hurries to finish, and when Lenny looks at the remaining questions he's annoyed at this inconvenience. He skims, marking off the answers randomly. He finishes the test, hands it in, and runs outside.

That night, while Lenny reads a new martial arts catalog, he hears his father tearing through the garage, tools clanking and boxes scraping the cement ground. He moves into the kitchen, opening and closing cabinets, and yells, "Where is the flashlight! I hate it when things aren't where they're supposed to be!"

Lenny suddenly realizes that he must have left the flashlight in the woods. He stands in his room, wondering what to do.

But then his mother returns home from work, and asks his father what's going on.

His father replies, and the only thing Lenny understands are the curses. Lenny peers out into the living room, and sees his father pointing to the garage. He totters off-balance. He whirls around and points his finger at Lenny. "Do you know where the flashlight is?"

"No," Lenny says.

"You are a liar. You always go through my tools."

"I don't know what you're talking about."

"Come here."

His mother steps forward and says something in Korean, something about her job. This distracts him. Lenny slips outside. He still feels weak from his bout with the flu, and doesn't want to stray too far. He climbs the maple tree, and settles into his favorite nook. He hears his parents arguing in the garage, and his mother says in English, "I found a job in four days." And then reverts to Korean.

Lenny hears her deriding tone; she's taunting him, comparing their job searches. Lenny doesn't like when she pushes him like that, but she does it so well that it only takes a few minutes for his father to become angry. He throws a roll of electrician's tape at her, missing her, and it bounces and rolls across the street.

His mother yells at him. "I can't wait until we divorce!"

His father comes out onto the front lawn and stands there for a moment. Then he looks up and sees Lenny.

His father asks where his sister is.

"At a friend's house."

His father says, "Come down and clean the tools up."

Lenny hesitates, not sure if his father could climb up here after him.

His repeats his command, and points to the tools and boxes in the garage.

Lenny says, "Why should I clean it? I didn't do that."

"B-Because I'm your father and I said so."

Tired and irritable, he says, "I don't want to."

His father puts his hands on his waist and stares. His body sways. Even in the dusk light Lenny can see his red face.

His father says, "All you do is hide up in the tree. You do b-bad tae kwon do and hide away from everything. This world is too hard to hide from. You have to face everything."

Lenny wants to retort, You don't face everything. You just get drunk every night. But Lenny keeps quiet. His father says, "Come down right now."

"No," Lenny replies.

"You stupid little b-boy, talking back to me? You show

me no respect? I will b-bring you down and show you respect." He makes a motion toward the tree, but then stops.
Lenny sees him calculating whether or not he can climb it.
He looks up at Lenny, and says, "You think you can be dis-
respectful like your mother? You learn b-bad things. Your
mother is making us lose our family. She is taking everything from me—"

He stops. He turns and goes into the garage, and Lenny
relaxes, thinking his father is going to fight with his mother,
but then his father reappears, and in the dim light he sees
that his father is carrying an ax.

PART IV

Wood Chips

27

Lenny sits up in the tree, watching with disbelief and fascination as his father walks across the front lawn with an ax in his hands. He's wearing khaki shorts, sandals, and an old tan Polo shirt with stains on the chest, and staggers drunkenly, almost tripping over his own feet. He yells at Lenny to come down, because he's going to chop down the tree. Lenny's mother jumps out of the front doorway, screaming at him to stay away from Lenny, and when he turns toward her, swaying, Lenny sees his chance, and scrambles down the tree, leaping to the ground and running.

His father tells her to shut up. He says, "No one respects me. No one! I work hard all d-day and no one gives me a chance! Not even my family! My own family!"

He picks up the ax and swings it back, but loses his grip. The ax slips out and spirals to the ground, sliding across the grass and leaving a pale green trail. He stumbles forward, reaching for it, and when he picks it up, Lenny has moved to the front door, where his mother pushes him inside. She says, "Go to your room."

But he hurries to the front window and sees his father gripping the ax with both hands, winding back, and then swinging with all his strength. The ax slices deeply into the trunk of the maple tree, and Lenny lets out a small cry. His father twists and pulls the handle, loosening the blade. Lenny says to his mother, "He's going to kill the tree!"

His father swings again, and the loud chop reverberates

through the front yard and into the house. Although Lenny
watches, he can't bear to see the tree hurt like that. He turns
away, and hears another chop. He remembers how he had
tried to hammer a piece of wood up in the branches as a
back rest, but when he saw that the nail had made the tree
bleed, he pulled it out and patched it with rubber cement.
He imagined the tree could feel this, and didn't want to hurt
it.

Now, after his father's fourth and fifth chop, he knows
the tree will die.

He sits on the sofa, staring at the large stereo with the
wood paneling. His mother closes the front screen door and
tells him to wash up for dinner. The chops outside continue, though the pace is slowing. After a few minutes Lenny
peers out the window and sees his father resting, and there
are deep gouges in the tree trunk, the dark bark chipped
away and the white fleshy core exposed. Large sweat stains
cover his father's back. The streetlamp flickers on, sending
a yellow glow over the lawn. For a moment it's eerily quiet.
A car drives by, slows down, but when Lenny's father glares
at it, the car speeds up.

His father wipes his forehead with his arm, and then
continues chopping the tree.

The slow, erratic chops—a physical, visceral sound that vi-
brates through the yard—imprint themselves in Lenny's
memory, and will be one of the last demonstrations of his father's strength and animosity. At one point his father takes
off his shirt, and in the darkness his thick, sweating body
glistens yellow under the streetlamp. His mother pushes
him away from the window and leads him to the kitch-

en, where she sets dinner in front of him. He eats alone in the breakfast nook, listening to the thunks that reverberate through the house.

The rhythm slows, the chops become quieter, and then, after a long pause, he hears a tremendous cracking and a heavy, resounding thud that shakes the house. Lenny and his mother run to the living room, and a blur of maple leaves and branches press up against the front window, blocking out the yellow streetlight. When his mother opens the front door a branch pops into the house, and there's a thick tangle of leaves blocking her. The bizarre image of a branch sticking through the door and into the living room almost makes Lenny laugh, but his mother angrily shoves aside the branch and pushes her way out the door, yelling at his father in Korean.

Lenny follows her through the branches and threads his way out onto the yard where the tree lies on its side. There are deep trenches in the lawn. The broken stump has white shards sticking out, with strips of twisted and tortured bark still attached to the fallen trunk. His mother says to his father something in Korean about the mess he's made, and he replies in a tired voice. He moves toward the branches jutting against the house, and chops those. He sees Lenny watching and says, "Go to bed."

"You killed my tree."

"Your tree? Your tree? This is my house, my yard. Go to b-bed now."

Lenny walks through the branches and back into the house. He hears his father chopping some of the smaller branches, the cracks higher in tone. As he gets ready for bed and settles into his room, listening to the rustling and snap-

ping of branches, he falls asleep and dreams of spiraling he-
licopter maple seeds falling around him.

When Lenny wakes up the house is quiet and still, and he
walks into the living room, which is unusually bright. He
looks out of the window and sees many of the large branches cut and piled in the corner of the yard. The huge trunk
still lies there in the center of the lawn, with long gashes in
the grass and large, leafy branches sticking up into the air,
but all the branches that were jutting against the house have
been pruned back. Wide, green maple leaves are scattered
everywhere. The yard seems brighter, airier.

Lenny walks out onto the lawn, his bare feet swishing
through the dew-covered grass. He sees the white wood
chips sprinkled across the yard and picks one up. He likes
the compactness of it, and when he realizes that this chip
was once part of his favorite tree, he puts it in his pajama
pocket. He finds a larger one and keeps it as well. He begins
collecting as many wood chips as he can, stuffing them in
his pocket, and when his pockets are full, using his pajama
top as a net.

His mother opens the front door and asks him what he's
doing.

"I want to save some of these."

She said his pajama bottoms are getting wet.

"I don't care."

She disappears for a moment, and then comes outside
with a plastic bag, and begins helping him collect the wood
chips. After she fills the bag she hands it to him, and tells
him to go inside and get ready for school. He brings the bag
into his room, sorts and dumps them into an empty shoe-

box. The chips will travel with Lenny for years, handfuls getting lost or misplaced with each move, but one day, in his late twenties, he will pull out the bag, choose an unblemished chip and begin whittling a pendant, which he still wears today.

Over the next few days his father and brother chop the tree into piles of firewood, and one of their neighbors with a gas-powered chain saw comes over to cut the stump and the few larger pieces of the tree trunk. The front yard seems empty. There used to be a birch tree in the other corner, but his father chopped that down when it began to die. Except for what's provided by a tall oak that borders the next-door neighbor's yard, they don't have any tree cover.

Lenny has to repair the gouges in the lawn, but his father seems too tired to keep hounding him about the yard work. His father is still in the midst of a job search, and although his mother hasn't revealed all the details yet, she is about to initiate divorce proceedings. Both of them are out often. Mira spends more time with friends and Lenny has the house to himself.

The mail-order pamphlets arrive during one of these solo afternoons, and he's disappointed that they're simply a bunch of mimeographed copies stapled together in a crude hand-made book. Even the staples are cheap and bent, misaligned in the spine. The copies are printed in the same purple ink of school ditto handouts.

However, once he reads the pamphlets more closely he sees that they are step-by-step directions for all phases of planting, growing, harvesting and drying marijuana, with line drawings. The detailed explanations are listed in simple, clear language. On the back of them is the name of the organization, a cooperative in Berkeley, California. Because Sal had paid for these, they are his, but Lenny brings them to the Merrick Library and photocopies a set for himself.

Excited by the arrival, Sal asks Lenny to water the crops while he stays at home to study these. After an initial glimpse, he hands Lenny more cash and says, "Find other catalogs and books. Stuff like this is great."

Lenny counts out fifty dollars. "About growing?"

"Anything. And keep the change again."

They're sitting in his crawlspace, and he pulls a small lamp closer to him. Lenny asks about the trip lines, even though they haven't seen any more evidence of trespassers.

"Keep them up. Maybe that one time was just some guy wandering around. I'm guessing it was night when he showed up, so maybe he didn't even notice the plants. But check everything carefully just in case."

"Come back here?"

He says, "I might be upstairs. You know what? Here's an extra key for the lock here. You can hang out here if you want. If you ever need to crash here, go ahead. Just make sure I'm not here, sleeping. I'm usually not, but just in case." He hands over a key to the padlock.

"Thanks."

"No big deal."

"Things okay at home?"

Lenny shrugs his shoulders.

Sal finally says, "Okay. Let me go through these. Thanks." He settles into a cushion, hunching over, and studies the pamphlets.

28

Lenny finds Ed that afternoon packing most of his belongings into the storage room, preparing for his summer off. Ed
asks how school is, and Lenny tells him about the stupid test
he hadn't understood.

Ed tilts his head. "I hope you did well."

"Why?"

"Those are placement tests for junior high school. You're
going to be tracked based on those tests."

"Tracked."

"You know: Gifted, Advanced, Regular, Dumbshit."

"What?" Lenny says, alarmed.

"Yeah, and you can't get off it. It tracks you into high
school, and your GPA gets added points if you're in the
higher tracks so the higher tracks get into better colleges. I
got fucked. So, I hope you did well."

Lenny says that he rushed through it quickly to get to
recess.

Ed raises an eyebrow. "Why did you do that?"

"I didn't know it was important!"

"Oh, man. You're going to be a dumbshit." He laughs.
"Just because you wanted to go play kickball!"

Lenny feels queasy.

His brother's goodbye is brief and uneventful. Mira and
Lenny hadn't gone to his graduation, and no one had gone
to Lenny's, including Lenny himself. He never gave his par-

ents the invitation, and he just didn't care. All these events make the end of the school year feel anti-climactic. When Ed leaves the house he hoists a heavy backpack over his shoulder, punches Lenny in the arm and says, "Catch you later." Their mother kisses him. Their father shakes his hand, and Ed ruffles Mira's hair.

Then he walks out of the house and jumps into his friend's Mustang. They screech off, and that's more or less the last Lenny sees of Ed for years. The strange thing is that there doesn't seem to be much of a difference in the house. He was there so rarely anyway, that for Lenny the biggest change is his new bedroom in the basement, where it's cold and damp, but completely private.

The back door leads directly to the basement stairwell, so Lenny often leaves and enters the house without seeing anyone. Lately, though, his mother has taken over the kitchen table in the breakfast nook for her work and studying, so sometimes Lenny finds her late at night preparing for her realtor exam.

One night he comes upstairs and finds her studying, charts and graphs of home prices in front of her, and she brightens when Lenny appears. She asks him to join her. She shows him her test preparation books, and tells him she likes this because it involves so many different areas, like math, reading, and even art and architecture. The test is in a couple of weeks, and she feels ready. She says, "I never thought I would become a real estate broker."

"You wanted to be a painter, didn't you?"

"Yes. Maybe I will go back to it eventually. What do you like to do?"

He thinks about the books, pamphlets and magazines,

and says, "I like to read."

"Maybe you can be a professor."

"Maybe."

"I don't give you a lot of advice, but I will say one thing. Find what you love and do it well and keep doing it, and the money will follow. If I had followed that advice maybe I would be a famous painter by now."

She touches his cheek. "I know you will do well. I can see it."

"How?"

"Because you never give up."

She kisses his forehead and tells him to go back to bed.

Sal has to go to summer school, but because Lenny has his days free, he cares for the crops, and he watches the plants grow taller and bushier, those with the premature flowers tagged as male—the tiny stalks and symmetrical knobs indicating their sex— appearing even larger and thicker. Sal wants to wait until the pre-flowering stage when the females begin clustering their new leaves, fully revealing their sexes, and then they'll decide what to do with the males.

Lenny studies the copies of the pamphlets as closely as Sal, and they debate the idea of fertilizing the females with male pollen to produce seeds for the next crop. Sal isn't sure if there will be another crop, and he still has plenty of seeds stored in his crawlspace. Although Lenny understands that female plants that don't make seeds are more potent, he keeps thinking about the future. Sal repeats a few times that growing in the woods is too hard. Lenny wonders about his attic and the backyard. Even though he doesn't know yet how complicated harvesting and drying is, and he has no idea about selling, it's the notion that he, a kid, could grow something illegal, coveted and profitable that appeals to him.

A couple of the catalogs advertise seeds for sale, though he isn't sure how legal this is and worries about his parents getting in trouble. He considers using another address, maybe his elderly neighbor's, making sure he intercepts her mail.

Lost in thought as he returns home, he's startled to find a strange Korean man sitting on the front steps, smoking a cigarette. He stands up when he sees Lenny, ducking his head shyly, and asks in broken and barely understandable English something about whose house this is.

He has large bags under his sad eyes, and his teeth are crooked and tobacco-stained. A belt holds up oversized jeans. Lenny asks him whom he's looking for, and the man says "Yul." Then he asks, "Are you Won Chul?"

That's Lenny's Korean name. He nods his head.

"I am Gil. Your…" He pauses, thinking of the word. "… uncle? I see you when you…" He lowers his hand to his thigh.

"You're my father's brother?" Lenny asks, not recognizing him.

He smiles and said he is.

He doesn't look like Yul, and because his parents had never mentioned a visit, Lenny is suspicious. He asks Gil to wait here while he calls his mother. Gil sits back down, and lights another cigarette.

Umee hadn't known Gil was coming, and tells Lenny she will call him back. After a few minutes his father calls, and asks to speak with Gil. Lenny hurries to the front door and opens it, motioning him in and leading him to the kitchen phone.

He speaks to Yul in Korean, and Lenny hears his father's voice asking curt questions. Uncle Gil replies in a soft, apologetic tone, and after a few minutes, he hands Lenny the phone.

His father says, "Keep an eye on him until I come home."

"What do you mean?"

"Just don't let him touch anything."

"How can I do that?"

"Just do it," his father says. "I will be home early." He hangs up.

Lenny turns to his uncle, and they stand there awkwardly for a minute. Lenny offers him a drink, which he doesn't understand, so Lenny motions drinking with his hand and Gil grins. "Yes, yes. Thank you."

Uncle Gil originally came to the U.S. on a tourist visa, which had expired years ago, and he's here illegally. He's in town now to ask his brother for a job.

Lenny doesn't understand much of what's going on, because unlike the conversations his parents have, which are often sprinkled with English, Gil and Yul speak quickly and without the same inflections. When Lenny asks his mother she tells him that his father is angry at this surprise visit and burden. "Your father always had to take care of Gil when they were younger, and he didn't like it."

"What can Gil do, if he's here illegally?"

"Many Korean storeowners can hire him off the books."

"How long will he stay with us?"

"Not long," she says. "Your father won't let him."

Gil smokes a lot, and Lenny often finds him sitting on the back steps, mashing out a cigarette in an old ceramic pot that quickly fills up with butts and matches. His English is limited to a few words, but they manage to communicate through gestures.

One afternoon Lenny asks him about his father, trying to find out what he was like as a kid. It takes a while, but Lenny finally conveys his question, and Gil sits and thinks about this while blowing smoke rings. He finally points to the house and makes a fist. "Abogee, daddy, uh…" He tries to think of a word, but shakes his head. Then Lenny gets an idea. He finds a Korean-English dictionary on his mother's bookshelf and hands it to Gil, who smiles. He flips through it and says, "Your daddy… tough."

Later, Lenny's mother explains more. She and Gil have talked, and she learns that Yul used to punish Gil by making him lift a wheelbarrow and carry it across the yard. If Gil dropped it he wouldn't be allowed to sleep in the house.

"Where was their father? Their mother?"

"Your grandfather was never home. He was a smuggler."

Lenny had forgotten about that, the stories of his grandfather smuggling opium into Korea. "And their mother?"

"I don't know. They don't talk about her very much. I think she was also hard on them. They were a hard family. You have to remember that about your father, how he is. It's all he knows."

Lenny can't imagine his father as a kid, but he can see Gil as a child, because of the tentative and awkward way he seems to deal with everyone, including Lenny. Gil has trouble looking people in the eye. He talks to peoples' feet, mumbling in a low voice. But his timidity annoys Yul, who barks at him, and Gil straightens his posture. Yul's tone is tinged with disgust whenever Lenny overhears him talking about his brother, and Lenny begins to feel sorry for Gil.

Handy with tools, Gil helps with a few household repairs, including fixing the garage door, which often sticks, and cleaning out the gutters. Yul inspects these the same way he inspects Lenny's yard work—Lenny notices a similar glimmer of hostility in Gil's eyes.

One afternoon Lenny hears them arguing in the garage. Gil's voice is characteristically quiet and subdued, but there's an edge to it, an insistence that angers his father, who speaks in clipped tones. Lenny doesn't know what they're saying, but Gil loses his temper, raising his voice.

Yul replies, and Lenny hears the garage door opening. His father storms back to the house, gathers Gil's bag and clothes, and throws them out the front door. His father then sits in the living room and turns on the stereo. Lenny goes outside through the garage and sees Gil picking up his clothes and packing them angrily in the small duffel bag. His face is flushed. When he sees Lenny he takes a deep breath, and lights up a cigarette. He asks, "Taxi? Bus? Where?"

"You can get one at the train station," Lenny says, pointing beyond the church. "Train."

Gil nods his head, understanding. He hesitates. He sticks out his hand to shake. "Goodbye," he says.

"Goodbye." Lenny shakes his hand, which is covered in rough calluses.

Gil inhales the cigarette, turns and walks down the street. Lenny never sees him again.

29

Umee passes the real estate broker exam, but continues to work as a receptionist and secretary while she trains with her boss. Yul, pleased for her, celebrates with a bottle of wine with dinner, imagining aloud that she will tap into the Korean market and then set up her own firm in New York, where rich Koreans will use her services to buy investment property.

But Umee quickly dismisses this, saying that all she wants is a good, steady job.

"No vision, no d-dreams," Yul says scornfully.

"Like a candy store in the middle of nowhere?"

They are eating at the kitchen table, and the small radio on the shelf plays the local classical station. Everyone falls quiet as Yul considers this retort. The announcer on the station comes on in his soothing, deep voice, and Mira and Lenny exchange glances. They know they will be leaving the table any minute.

Yul says, "It would've worked if the economy was b-better and you did a b-better job."

Umee then does something uncharacteristic. Lenny expects her to spit something back, or to shut down, but instead she puts her glass of wine carefully on the table and looks coolly at Yul. She says, "Blame me all you want. Everyone knows the truth." She motions her head toward the kids, which surprises Lenny.

Yul reverts to Korean, his voice threatening. But Umee

isn't fazed. She shrugs a shoulder and replies. Her reaction also seems to confuse Yul, and when Mira and Lenny ask to be excused he waves them away. Yul and Umee begin to talk quietly in Korean, and the strength with which Umee handles her husband is so interesting to Lenny that he sits on the steps to the basement, the door closed, so he can eavesdrop. He doesn't know precisely what they're saying, but his mother seems to be laying out an argument slowly and carefully, bullet points for his father to consider. His father listens for a while and then replies in a tired voice. Lenny hears his father's chair scraping the floor as he leaves the table. He walks to the bedroom and closes the door.

Lenny emerges from the basement stairwell as his mother clears the table. He asks her what happened. She blinks rapidly, her expression disbelieving. She says, "I told him I hired a divorce lawyer. I want him to move out soon."

Based on the advice in the pamphlets, Sal and Lenny harvest some leaves and growing shoots. Although the main goal is the final harvest, especially the buds, which is approaching more quickly that Sal had thought—the ideal weather, the swampy soil, and the strain of cannabis all contribute to this—Sal needs to sample some of the new growths for the potency. He dries the leaves in his oven when his parents aren't home, and rolls a joint. Because he's worried about the smell, he smokes it in the woods. He says, "I'd offer you some, but I think you're too young."

"I think I should try a little."

He hands Lenny the joint, who never smoked anything before, and because of his soft palate problems he has trouble inhaling without leaking air in through his nose. Sal laughs at his difficulty, and finally Lenny holds his nose to suck in the smoke. It burns his throat, and he has a coughing fit.

"I know. It could be smoother."

"People do this for fun?" Lenny gags.

"A bong would cool off the smoke, but the leaves are harsh. I'm going to experiment with curing, because that's supposed to help. Slow drying too."

Lenny's eyes water, and he hands the joint back to him. "I don't feel anything."

"You probably won't, not the first few times. I'm feeling it."

Lenny studies him. He seems no different than usual. It occurs to him that maybe Sal is often stoned. They sit on the edge of the concrete run-off, a small stream of water splashing into the creek, brown and yolk-colored foam congealing near their feet. The sweetness of the marijuana covers up the rot smell of the swamp.

He tells Lenny he's found the model of motorcycle he wants, and will probably buy it used, once he sells the bulk of the crop. He says, "I already have buyers for most of it. Not guaranteed or anything, but I know a bunch of dealers who can handle a quarter or half pound."

They haven't talked about Lenny's payment since he first started working with Sal. Lenny says, "I've done a lot so far."

Sal smiles and nods his head. "Your base payment is still three hundred dollars, but there's going to be a bonus, no doubt. It all depends on how much usable weed we harvest and how much I can get for it. I promise you that I won't screw you over. Just with the mail order stuff you've probably helped me make better weed."

"Okay."

"You're going to have a lot of cash for a kid. What are you going to do with it?"

"Save it. Most of it."

"Good. You should open a bank account. Do you have one?"

"My father opened one for me. There's only twenty dollars in it."

"Watch out for that. My friend had a joint account with his dad, and his dad emptied it out."

Lenny didn't think of that.

Sal says, "I also want a small boat. I'm thinking about taking a boat license course. You want to take one with me?"

"Maybe."

"It's to certify us to pilot a boat without adults. They're giving the course at the Freeport Recreation center. Think about it."

They sit quietly while Sal continues smoking his joint.

Lenny tells him that his parents are getting a divorce.

"Oh, man. You going to move or what?"

"I don't know."

"Here. Try another hit." He hands Lenny the joint. This time Lenny sucks the smoke into his mouth, and then inhales that with air, and it goes down more smoothly. He still coughs, but not as badly.

Lenny passes the joint back. They hear the cars on Sunrise Highway above them, the babbling water below, and as he takes a deep hit, the ember sizzling, Lenny hears a train approaching. He finds a sense of calm settling through him.

Lenny sighs contentedly.

Sal says, "Yup."

Lenny still does the yard work at the house to pay for the
dent repair, but after well over a month of this he suspects
his father is taking advantage of him. His father wakes Lenny up in the morning with a list of tasks, including mowing
the lawn, trimming the hedges, and weeding the grassy area
along the sidewalk. Lenny tells him he mowed last week,
and his father says, "The lawn grows. Time to mow it again."

"I think I've paid for the dent by now."

"I don't think so."

"How much did it cost?"

"Two hundred dollars."

"I've mowed and trimmed and weeded and raked twice
a week for a month and a half, even more. I think I've paid
for it."

"Now that Ed is gone, you are responsible for the yard."

"Why don't you do it?"

He says, "You stupid little b-boy. You will do what I say."

Lenny sits on his bed. His father put his hands on his
hips, waiting for a response. Lenny wonders what his life
will be like when his parents split up. He says, "I am going
to call up landscaping businesses to find out how much they
charge. If it looks like I've done more than $200 of work,
then I am going to start charging you."

His father is about to reply, but stops. He smiles. "You
are getting smarter. That's good b-business sense. Starting
next week if you take care of all the yard work I will p-pay
you an allowance."

"How much?"

"Three dollars a week."

"That's all?"

"If you p-pass inspection and I don't have to remind you every time, then four dollars a week."

"How about five?"

"Don't get greedy."

His sister tells him of a garage sale nearby, so they go together that afternoon, and while she searches for a new record player Lenny examines one of two TV's for sale—an old black and white, and a small color TV. Neither is right for his room, but while browsing the books he finds a bin full of *Radio Electronics* and *Popular Science* magazines. In one issue of *Radio Electronics* are plans, including a parts list and detailed instructions, for how to build a telephone eavesdropping device. His heart starts beating quickly. The older woman tending the sale wears a flowing glittery wrap and scarf, her hair beaded. She lookes surprised that Lenny wants to buy a box of magazines, and accepts his offer for two dollars. She says, "You Orientals like engineering, I guess."

This startles him. He doesn't know how to reply to that, and just hands her the two dollars. Mira is disappointed that there's nothing for her to buy.

But when they return home she surprises him with a gift. It's a small smooth rock that has been painted yellow, with a face of a bear on the front. "What is it?" he asks.

"Pet rock."

"You paid for this?"

"A dollar."

"You paid a dollar for a rock? Are you joking?"

She blinks, her expression hurt. "It's a present."

"How could you waste money like that?" He's about to

throw the rock out the window, but stops. Mira looks like she's about to cry. He realizes how mean he's being and quickly says, "You know what? It's cool. I like it. Thanks."

"I got it for you."

"I know. It's great. I'm sorry. I like it a lot. Really I do."

She turns away without speaking and walks to her room.

Lenny holds the rock in his hand, cursing himself for not being more thoughtful. He vows to keep this rock forever and make sure he's careful about other peoples' feelings. He looks at the bear and says, "You will keep me from being mean."

30

Harvest time for the marijuana coincides with Lenny's father's fading from their lives. Sal has already taken the males, cutting them down before their flowers open, but now the females are in full bloom; according to the pamphlets the buds are their most potent as the flowering slows, so it's time. Sal dries the males in the crawlspace, but he worries he doesn't have enough room for the more important females. The males hang upside down on string, a small fan blowing air around them to prevent molding.

They work at night, because they have to carry three heavy burlap bags, large and suspicious looking. Sal has a make-shift trailer—just a large piece of plywood with baby-stroller wheels attached—that he hooks onto the back of his minibike, and they tie down the bags with bungie cords.

It's three in the morning, and both of them are exhausted from cutting and carrying the plants through the woods, worrying about cops. He starts up the engine, and they cringe at the noise. He says, "Hurry up. Get on."

Lenny climbs onto the back, and Sal pulls forward, glancing over his shoulder at the trailer. It shudders and clatters behind them, but seems secure. Sal tells Lenny to keep a sharp lookout, but the streets are empty. He speeds back to his house, killing the engine before he reaches the driveway, and they coast into his back yard. Moving quickly, they bring the three huge burlap bags into this crawlspace, though there really isn't any room. The drying males crisscross the low ceiling, and the smell makes Lenny's eyes water.

"We'll leave this here and deal with it tomorrow," Sal says, opening the burlap bags to air the plants out.

"How will you dry all this?"

"Do you think we can use your attic?"

Lenny hesitates. "I don't know."

"You said no one goes up there."

"But getting it there will be hard. My mom stays up late in the kitchen, and my sister is around a lot."

"You can do it a little at a time. It's going to take a couple weeks to dry all this out anyway. Every day just bring a few plants, string them up to dry. Make sure there's ventilation."

"There is. It still gets hot up there, though."

"Start tonight. Be really careful with these. The oils on here have all the THC. If they get rubbed off, we lose it." He carefully wraps three plants in cheesecloth, and hand them to Lenny, who is too tired to argue. He cradles them in his arms, and walks home.

The moon shines brightly down as he presses his nose close to the plants and inhales them. The sweet smell has become familiar and comforting to him. Although he has smoked some more since that first time, he doesn't particularly like it, especially since it seems to aggravate his allergies, and inhaling is difficult with his nasal problems. It also does something strange to the back of his eyeballs, making them feel as if they're bulging. But he likes the idea that he can grow something natural and sell it for money.

Instead of bringing the plants into the attic in the middle of the night, which he knows will make noise throughout the house, he strings them up in his closet, throwing his coats and shirts onto the floor. Tomorrow he'll figure out how to use the attic once everyone goes to work. Maybe he'll send his sister on an errand to keep her out of the house.

Lenny looks at the clock: it's almost four a.m. He's so tired he collapses on his bed in his clothes, the smell of marijuana on his fingertips, and falls asleep.

Lenny's mother gives him updates about the impending divorce—Yul hired a lawyer, and they're negotiating the terms, including the division of property, assets and the house. Umee just wants out of the marriage, so she surrenders more than she should have. She's close to selling her first house as a newly minted Real Estate Broker, and is confident that she can support her children without their father. But she worries about their college fund. "I will fight for that," she tells Lenny.

But his father still lives at home, and the strange détente that exists between them gives the house a muted, awkward feel. Lenny's mother spends most of her time at the kitchen table, while his father stays out of the house, sometimes for a couple of days at a time. When he returns, he drinks in the living room and then slumps off to bed. Lenny's mother sleeps on the sofa.

Yul becomes morose and withdrawn, but it's the knowledge of his departure that emboldens Lenny. He no longer maintains the yard, and when his father tells Lenny that he isn't going to pay the agreed allowance, Lenny shrugs it off. When his father asks Lenny to shine his shoes, Lenny refuses. His father looks as if he's about to yell, but after a moment stops himself. He turns away without saying anything.

He leaves boxes of files and computer books stacked in
the basement office as he slowly packs his belongings. Lenny snoops through the paperwork and amidst the bills and
delinquent notices, he finds a file of receipts, including one
from an auto body shop for a dent repair, dated shortly after
Lenny dinged the car with the ladder. The total cost for the
repair was sixty-five dollars. Lenny studies this, angry that
his father had lied about the cost of the repair and made
Lenny work more than he should have. Lenny wants to con-
front his father with it, but knows he's drunk right now.

Lenny walks up into the kitchen, stewing at the fact that
he'd been cheated by his own father, when he calls out to
Lenny, telling him to bring some ice. Lenny ignores him. He
calls Lenny again, and Lenny says, "Get it yourself."

Lenny hears him move off the couch and walk toward
the kitchen. Lenny slips out through the garage, and hurries
along the side of the house, hearing him call out again.

He appears in the front doorway as Lenny crosses the
street. He yells to come back.

"No," Lenny says. "I know you lied to me about the dent.
It didn't cost two hundred dollars. It was only sixty-five dollars. You made me work more than I had to."

His father thinks about this, swaying. He says, "How did
you know that?"

"I saw the receipt."

"You should not be going into my files!"

"You shouldn't be lying to me and cheating me. You owe
me money."

"How dare you talk to me like that!" He lets out a string
of Korean curses. "You come back right now!"

Lenny stares at his father, whose face is sweaty and red.

He has to hold onto the doorframe for support. Lenny is completely disgusted.

"Then you stay out! You don't come back here."

"Fine," Lenny says, walking away.

"Don't come back!"

"I won't!"

Lenny moves down the street, heading toward the library. He considers staying out as long as he can, sleeping in Sal's crawlspace. He regrets not telling his father how he really feels, how glad he is about the divorce.

He then hears someone call his name. He turns around. It's Mira on her small bicycle, streamers flowing from her handlebars and a wicker basket in front with a sunflower design. She calls out to him again and tells him to wait up. He stops, puzzled.

She rides up to him, her feet pedaling quickly. She's out of breath.

"What do you want?"

"Where are you going?"

"Away."

Her eyes widen. "You're leaving?"

"He kicked me out."

She looks down, and finally says, "I want to go with you."

Lenny, taken aback, says, "I'm not really leaving. I'll be back. Go home." He starts to walk away, and she follows him. He turns to her. "What are you doing?"

"I want to go with you."

"I'm just going to the library."

"I want to go too."

He sighs. "All right. Come on."

She rides next to him, her wheels squeaking.

The next afternoon Lenny receives a letter in the mail from Merrick Avenue Junior High School, telling him that he placed in the regular classes, and the schedules will be sent to him in a month. He completely forgot about this, about taking that test, and now he wonders if he should tell his mother.

He calls her at work, and she answers the phone in her secretary's voice. When he explains what happened with the test and the results of that, she practically yells into the phone, "Why didn't you tell me earlier?"

"I forgot."

"You forgot that you ruined your academic career?"

"I didn't ruin—"

"Give me the phone number on the letter."

"Mom, it's no big deal—"

"Give me the number."

Sheepishly, he does. She hangs up without saying anything else. A few minutes later she calls back and says, "I'm picking you up in twenty minutes. We're meeting the vice principal."

"Now?"

"Twenty minutes." She hangs up.

Twenty minutes later his mother picks him up, telling him that she had to take off from work, and this is something he should've told her about as soon as it happened. She says, "You understand what this means, don't you?"

"The tracking? Ed told me."

"You told Ed, but you didn't tell me?"

"I forgot."

She shakes her head angrily. "This is not a joke. This is your future."

He rarely sees her this angry at him, and he sinks down into his seat. When they arrive at the school, which is open for summer school but mostly empty, they walk into the administration offices, where Mr. Jasper, the Vice Principal, is waiting for them.

Mr. Jasper, tall and lanky, has a full beard and mustache, and speaks calmly to Umee about this unnecessary visit, because, as he stated on the phone, there isn't much he can do.

Lenny's mother launches into a long explanation of what happened with her son, why his test scores are low, and, based on his grades, why he should be in the gifted program.

"I'm afraid the scores determine—"

"Then he should retake the test."

"That's impossible. We don't make the tests. They're state-administered, and anyway, if everyone could retake the test it would be—"

"I am not talking about everyone. I am talking about my son."

"He can start out in regular classes and his teachers can recommend his being bumped up to advanced—"

"But he will already be behind. This can't be. I will not let this happen. I will take him to private school if I have to. I will contact the newspapers and the ACLU and the Korean Legal Aid to let them know that this tracking is unfair and is a form of discrimination!" Her voice cracks and Lenny sees that her cheeks are red, her hands shaking.

Mr. Jasper says quickly, "That's not necessary. Your son

is obviously a good student. Look, I can arrange to have him in advanced classes, because those aren't just test-based, but he can't go into the gifted classes. And if his average falls below ninety at any point we can put him back in regular."

She considers this, then nods her head. "Fine."

They leave, and as they walk back to the car, she says, "You better not let me down, Lenny."

"I won't. I promise."

She gives him a hard look.

He says, "Really. I won't." For the first time he understands how important she considers his schooling, and he vows that he will never let her down again.

31

Over the next two weeks Lenny manages to smuggle a half dozen more plants into his attic, hanging them to dry, while Sal prepares the rest. He tells Lenny the males are treated differently, especially the flowers, because they aren't as potent, and he makes small rolled sticks out of them. The females, especially their buds, once dried, will be the main source of potency.

He says he lined up buyers, using most of his original contacts. He tells Lenny this while pacing back and forth in his backyard, his fingers nervously tapping his leg. "This is stressful, man," he says. "Some of them want to sample it, but it's not ready. But they trust me because I've dealt with them in the past. But now I've got a reputation to keep up, so this has got to be smooth stuff. It's not like I'm just a middleman. I'm a source."

"How do you know them?"

"For a while I'd buy a quarter pound, maybe a half pound, and then dime bag it, sell it off and make a good profit. I got to know some dealers." He sits down, tapping his feet, and then stands up and paces again. "It's this waiting that's driving me nuts."

"You can use the oven again."

"No, that makes it too harsh. Just another week or so, and it'll be ready. You're making sure your attic is ventilated, right? Checking for mold?"

"Every day."

"Good. Good." He turns to Lenny. "I don't think I can
do this again. It's too much. I might just go back to regular
dealing."

"But the money."

"I'm not a minor anymore. This is serious shit if I get
caught."

Lenny nods. Over the past few weeks he witnessed Sal
get more and more nervous, and Sal confessed that he's
having trouble sleeping with the plants drying in his crawlspace. He keeps the door padlocked, and his parents never
go down there, but his younger sister is always snooping,
and the smell is beginning to rise up into the house. "Maybe
it's my imagination, but I keep smelling it everywhere. My
parents aren't dumb. They're going to figure it out unless I
bag and seal it soon."

"Just a few more days," Lenny says.

"Yeah. I know. I know."

Lenny's mother tells him they're going to keep the house,
take over the mortgage payments, and she will pay a lump
sum of twenty thousand dollars to his father. When Lenny
asks where she will get the money, she confides to him that
she has been saving money in secret for years, and will also
ask her mother and family for a loan. However, when Yul
realizes how quickly Umee agrees to these terms, he adds
a last-minute stipulation: if and when she sells the house
she'll also pay him another lump sum of ten thousand. Umee
just wants out and agrees. Yul will also pay two hundred a
month for child support and alimony until Lenny and Mira
turn eighteen. The details of the divorce seem straightfor-
ward, and are nothing like Lenny imagined. It's a business

deal. He's not sure why they didn't negotiate an end to the marriage much earlier.

His mother now works ten to twelve hours a day, not only to pay her family back for their loan, but also to pay the mortgage, now solely her responsibility. She is also taking classes and studying to be an appraiser. She tells Lenny that working as a real estate appraiser, especially for commercial property, means a steady and well-paying job regardless of the economy, unlike selling residential real estate.

One night she comes home, excited, and shows Lenny her first commission check for a house she just sold. The check, for over four thousand dollars, is wrinkled from her constantly pulling it out and reading it. She says, "My boss says he's never seen anyone take to this like me."

"Wow," Lenny says, but he thinks about how much Sal might make from selling his pot. One pound of pot can sell wholesale for over three thousand. If he dime bags it he'll get over four thousand, and this is just for growing a weed. Then again, Lenny's mother doesn't have to worry about getting arrested.

Sal, who grades and sorts the crop into quarter- and half-pound bags, warns Lenny again about telling anyone what's happening. They're now moving into the selling phase, and this makes Sal tense. The first of his deals is with his friend Tommy, who's curious to meet Lenny, the kid assistant who knows how to find information on growing techniques, so Lenny accompanies Sal to Tommy's house in East Meadow, near Eisenhower Park. They take the bus up Merrick Avenue, and look like any two kids heading to the park, though Sal has a backpack full of marijuana.

Tommy lives in a split-level white house with a lush

green lawn. Assorted flower windmills sit in the garden, though none of them spin in the stagnant heat. They walk up to the front door and ring the bell. A woman in her sixties, wearing a tank top, her shoulders freckled and brown, opens the door. Sal greets her, asking if her grandson is in. She calls upstairs to Tommy and lets them walk upstairs.

Tommy opens his bedroom door. It's a teen's room, with Pink Floyd, Queen and David Bowie posters covering the walls. Sal asks Tommy why he's not with his brother.

Tommy smiles. "Got kicked out. Now it's grandma time."

He turns up the stereo and locks his door. He looks at Lenny and says, "So this is the kid."

Sal introduces them.

Tommy studies Lenny and says, "Does he speak English?"

Sal and Lenny glance at each other, and Sal laughs. "Of course he does."

"Of course I do," Lenny says.

Tommy has long, messy hair, brown curls falling over his face, and a leather wrist band that slides up his arm when he pushes back his hair. He says, "Sal showed me the books you got. Nice. You getting more?"

"I'm trying."

"Cool." He turns to Sal. "The samples were good. You got the half?"

Sal reaches into his back pack and pulls out a large football-shaped bag of marijuana, clear plastic tape wrapped tightly around it. He hands it to Tommy.

"Hell, why'd you tape it up so much?"

"I was worried about the smell."

Tommy weighs the package on a small spring-loaded postal scale on his desk. He nods and pulls out a wad of cash, counting out $900, laying the bills on the desk. Sal takes it, thanks him, and they talk for a while about a guy they know who bought a pound of pot to sell but ended up smoking all of it himself. They laugh. Tommy looks at Lenny and says, "Can you see out of those slanted eyes?"

Lenny, confused, says, "Yes."

Sal says to Tommy, "Yo."

Tommy asks Sal, "How do you blindfold a chink?"

"Come on, man," Sal says.

"With dental floss."

"Hey, hey," Sal says. "That's not cool."

"He knows I'm just kidding. Right, Bruce Lee?"

Lenny doesn't want to mess up Sal's deal, so he doesn't respond.

"Can you really speak English?" Tommy asks.

"Yes, I can." Lenny turns to Sal and says, "I'll wait outside for you."

As he walks downstairs he hears Sal tell Tommy, "That wasn't cool, man."

"What's the big deal?"

Outside Lenny sits on the front steps and watches one of the neighbors washing his car. When Sal comes out he motions for Lenny to follow him, and they walk back to the bus stop. He says, "He can be kind of an asshole."

"You only got nine hundred?"

"I cut him a deal because he got the seeds."

Lenny nods, but doesn't say much else. His opinion of Sal has fallen because he's friends with Tommy. While wait-

ing for the bus, Sal counts out $300 and hands it to Lenny.
"This is what I promised. There's another two hundred for
you after the next deal."

"I don't think I want to go with you."

"Yeah."

Lenny pockets the cash, and even though he knows it's
a lot, more than he's ever had before, he finds this whole
process disappointing. He thinks about buying a TV, about
saving the money for more books, but all this has been taint-
ed by Tommy's comments.

Lenny and Sal end up not talking for the rest of the way
back to Merrick, and when the bus drops them off at the
train station, Sal says he'll call in a couple days after the next
sale, and he'll have the money.

Lenny thanks him. Sal says the next time they see each
other Sal will be on his new motorcycle.

"I'll give you a ride."

"Cool," Lenny says, and walks away.

Over the next few day Lenny begins searching for a good
color TV, visiting garage sales and the Sunrise mall. He also
buys supplies from Radio Shack—coaxial cable, splitters,
wire cutters—and studies the cable TV lines running along
the telephone poles. His plan is to steal a tag from another
pole and attach it to the illegal line he'll install to his house.
He also mail-ordered the plans and parts for a descrambler,
which will allow him to get all the premium pay channels.
In order to build this, though, he needs more equipment,
like a soldering iron, a volt- and ohmmeter, and various
wire crimping tools. He studies the plans and realizes he
needs a better understanding of circuit boards, and begins

spending hours in the library, teaching himself basic circuitry and soldering.

One afternoon as he walks back from Radio Shack he sees Sal on a large Kawasaki motorcycle speeding down Sunrise Highway. Lenny waves to him, and he pulls over, his hair windblown and tangled. "Check it out," he says.

"Looks great."

"Glad I ran into you." He reaches into his jacket and counts out two hundred dollars. "This is for you. Thanks for everything."

"You've been selling?"

"Almost all of it. I'm saving a half pound, but everything else is going for top dollar. I can finally sleep." He smiles, his underbite jutting forward.

"Are you going to grow again?"

"I don't think so, at least not for the next season. I have all those seeds, but I think I can store them for a year. But thanks for your help."

"Thanks for this." Lenny holds up the cash.

Sal revs his bike, and says goodbye, speeding off into traffic.

Lenny walks home with the roll of twenties in his pocket, worried to have this and the $260 left in his room. He remembers what Sal said about joint bank accounts, and he doesn't trust his father to have access to the money, so he considers asking his mother to open an account for him.

When he walks into the house, he sees boxes stacked in the garage, and then hears his father's drunken voice say, "You ruined my family!"

He stops, turns around, and creeps quietly across the street to the church.

32

Yul is supposed to be moving out this weekend, and although he begins the process of loading his Cadillac, he starts drinking in the morning and is plastered by the afternoon. Lenny stays away from the house as long as he can, but gets hungry around dinnertime.

The kitchen, in shambles, has dishes, pots and pans strewn across the floor. Mira and his mother have locked themselves in Mira's room. His father is sprawled on the living room floor, and moans about how everything he worked for is disappearing. Lenny walks quietly to Mira's room, checking on them, and his mother unlocks the door. "Where were you?" she asks.

"With Sal. Is there dinner?"

His mother listens for a moment, then says she'll make something. Lenny follows her past the living room, where his father pulls himself up and says something in Korean. His mother ignores him.

In the kitchen, his mother picks up the pots and pans, and he helps her sweep the broken dishes into a dustpan. His father appears in the doorway, and he says, "Your mother is ruining this family!"

His mother says, "You ruined this family many years ago."

"You can't take my children away from me!"

Lenny, surprised by this, never thought his father was interested in his children except for doing chores. His father says, "All my life I tried to make a good family. I tried to give you all what I never had, and this is what happens?"

His mother says something sharp in Korean, and his father flinches.

His father replies in a mournful voice, and looks down at his bare feet. Lenny and his mother wait for a moment, but his father doesn't say anything else. Instead he walks quietly back into the living room and turns on the stereo.

His mother reheats leftovers and sets the kitchen table. Lenny watches her move briskly from the refrigerator to the stove as she stir-fries cold noodles and microwaves a tofu and beef dish. Mira walks into the kitchen and takes a seat next to him. She tells him she still hasn't found a record player to replace her broken one, and he says he'll help her look tomorrow, since he has to find a TV.

His father yells something from the living room. Mira glances at Lenny, her gaze uneasy. His mother yells back. There's a tremendous crash and pop that shakes the walls. His mother runs into the living room, and screams at him. Mira and Lenny walk out and see the huge stereo face down on the carpet, the wires and torn mesh fabric on the back exposed. His father looks down at it blearily. Some of the records have spilled out of a side pocket and fan out of their sleeves. The turntable still spins and clicks, but then stops.

His mother yells something, and he replies, "I don't want it anyway."

"It is time for you to leave," she says quietly, in English. "Our agreement is that you leave this house today."

He nods his head. "I am almost finished."

"Go."

His expression tightens and he looks as if he's going to

argue, but Lenny's mother cuts him off with, "This house belongs to me today. Do you really want me to call the police?"

"You would call the police on me?"

"I should've called the police years ago when you started beating me." His mother has a calm expression. She's utterly confident and unafraid. Lenny has never seen her like this before.

His father stares at her, then glances at Mira and Lenny. He then mutters something under his breath as he goes to put on his shoes.

Mira and Lenny eat quickly, and leave the house. They want to sneak into the church, but see the front office lit up. They peer over the bushes and spy the pastor on the telephone. He wears a sweater vest, his chubby, pale face bright under the fluorescent lights, and he rubs his forehead while he talks, a red welt forming over his eyes. This is the minister who came here after the former one had an affair with his secretary and divorced his wife. Mira and Lenny have never met this one. They walk to the side of the church, and sit on top of a wooden fence that borders an elderly woman's house. Her sidewalks are rusty brown from her old sprinkler system.

Mira asks, "Where is he going to live?"

They watch their father load his Cadillac with more boxes. He then lugs a huge suitcase, and throws it into the back seat. Lenny says, "I think he'll be in Flushing. Mom said he might have a new job at a bank in Queens."

"Will we see him again?"

"I have no idea."

As he carries another box, the bottom breaks. Computer paper falls out and tumbles down the driveway, the perforated sheets unfolding. The wind lifts a long section of it, spreading it farther across the sidewalk. Lenny's father drops the box and kicks the stack of paper, the long sheets extending and fluttering onto the lawn. After a moment he stares at the paper, picks it all up and dumps it into the garbage.

It's getting darker, and they see the pastor locking up and leaving the office. He walks across the lawn to his house next door. Mira and Lenny hurry to the back entrance and jimmy the door open. They move quickly through the dark, quiet halls and onto the stage of the back room. Lenny remembers the steeple and searches for the entrance up there while Mira stands on the stage and asks him to turn on the spotlights.

"Not yet. Just in case the minister comes back."

She speaks to her imagined audience, telling them that this next song is dedicated to her fans.

When Lenny climbs down from the back of the stage and into a small stairwell, he sees a narrow built-in ladder that leads up to a panel in the ceiling, very much like his own attic entrance. He can't find a light switch, so he climbs in the dark, using the smooth walls to guide him. The higher he climbs the warmer it becomes, but when he finds a handle and pushes open the ceiling door, he immediately feels the night breeze blowing around him. He calls down to his sister.

"What is it?" she says.

"I found the tower."

"I don't want to go up there. I'm afraid of bats."

"All right. You stay down there." He pulls himself up into the tower, and sees the wooden beam crisscrossing above, but there's no bell—two large bullhorns bolted to the beams connect to a tape deck and amplifier. Lenny moves closer to one of the ledges, the guardrail dusty and dirty. His sister calls to him, asking him what's up there.

"Not much. But there are no bats. Come up. Be careful."

She climbs up and clutches one of the large support beams in the center, peering cautiously down onto the street. A strong cold gust blows through here, and she says she's cold. Then Lenny points to the house, the garage light on and their father still loading his car. They see more lights turning on inside and outside the house. Their father can't close the trunk lid, so ties it down with string. He then walks out onto the sidewalk, looking around. He calls Lenny and Mira's name.

Mira says, "Should we answer?"

He shakes his head. Lenny knows his father wants to say goodbye. Their father puts his hands on his hips and calls to them again, shouting toward the church. At one point he looks up, and Lenny pulls back slowly, although he doubts his father can see them.

Lenny asks Mira if she remembers how he wanted them to perform in a talent show at this church. She doesn't.

For a brief time they all went to this church. When they first moved there the minister, Reverend Ames, and his wife welcomed their family with apple pie and an invitation to attend Sunday service. The Ames' had four children, the youngest about Ed's age, and all of them treated Lenny and his sister as cute, huggable babies, which he didn't mind, coming from the two daughters.

Reverend Ames and his wife were calm, quiet-spoken, and seemed to Lenny possessed of a New England reserve and charm that was foreign to him. He never saw them raise their voices or even give any of their children dirty looks. Everyone seemed unnaturally well-behaved.

This model family undoubtedly served as a nagging comparison to the Changs, and when there was a church talent show and potluck dinner, and some of the families were planning on performing, Lenny heard the envy in his father's voice as he told them that he wanted the family to do something. None of them had any real demonstrable talent, so his father wanted them to get on stage and sing a song together. He wanted them to sing "Edelweiss," from The Sound of Music, and, again, Lenny knew that the idyllic image of the Von Trapp family was serving as a template in his imagination, but unfortunately none of them could sing.

Ed flatly refused, and since he hadn't been going to church anyway, and everyone knew he would just disappear if he was required to be there, their father didn't press him. But then his mother said she didn't want to get on stage. None of them knew how to play the guitar, and she'd have to learn the piano accompaniment, which she didn't have time for. Their father looked at Mira and Lenny, and Lenny said that if Ed and Mom weren't going on stage, then he wasn't. They turned to Mira, who had a gleam in her eye, but their father then sighed and said never mind.

None of them went to the talent show, and their father brooded for days. Lenny heard him arguing with his mother in Korean, his frustration at the family directed at her. But even as a kid, Lenny knows that the fault lies not with her, and not even directly with him. This is a family that wants out. His father dreams of the sea. His mother dreams of freedom. Ed already has been making excursions away. It's only a matter of time before Lenny and Mira begin planning their escapes.

And as Mira and Lenny watch their father call out their names again, his voice hoarse and weaker, Lenny says, "He's getting ready to leave."

Mira is quiet. Their father calls out one more time and seems deflated. He drops his arms and walks slowly back to his car. Lenny knows all he has to do is go down there and say goodbye, but there's a hardness in him that wants to punish his father in any way he can, and that means not saying goodbye.

Mira and Lenny watch him look around for another minute. He then climbs slowly into his car and starts the loud, rumbling engine. Black smoke spews from the tailpipe. He backs down the driveway, the muffler bottoming out because of the weight of the boxes. The brakes squeal. He pulls into the street and, after revving the engine to warm it up, he drives down the street and turns the corner, the rumbling engine echoing and fading away.

PART V

A Sonata in Sunlight

33

Yul is such a gravitational force in the family that the orbits spin in unexpected and strange directions after his departure. Umee, now the sole provider, works many extra hours preparing for her real estate appraiser exam. She wakes up before dawn—her steps creaking above Lenny's ceiling—and studies in her home office until she heads to the real estate firm. Then, when she returns at seven or eight, she eats a quick dinner at her desk and continues working until well past midnight.

Over the next few weeks they begin leading lives that rarely intersect. Mira stays over at her friends' houses, and Lenny works on his various projects. He sets up in his room a small color TV that he bought from a pawnshop in Massapequa, and hooks up the illegal cable line. It's surprisingly easy: one night he simply brings the ladder out to the telephone pole and connects the coaxial cable to the splitter box. Then he takes a registration tag from another box down the street and attaches the tag to his line.

He doesn't even need a descrambler, because all the channels, including one premium channel, come in unscrambled. He finds, to his delight, more Asian imported Kung-Fu flicks.

He also continues reading up on different methods of marijuana cultivation, and studies his attic, the basement, and the back yard for possible growing sites. It's too late to start a new crop—the best time to begin is after the first frost—and he understands why Sal chose the remote swamp. But Lenny also critiques Sal's limiting the size—Sal could've spread out the plots and doubled or even tripled the number of plants. He could've also just dispersed the seeds randomly, and let the plants survive on their own, and then harvest them when they were ready. Despite this disorganization, it could've yielded more with less of a chance of being discovered.

All this is an academic exercise, because he doesn't think he'll grow anything on his own, especially because he's not sure how to get seeds. But he likes the problem-solving nature of this, and he even decides to check the pH level of the backyard soil by buying pH test kits from a gardening store. Dissolving sample soil into a test tube with a special solution and comparing the color to a chart, he finds that his soil is slightly acidic. To make the soil more alkaline he needs to add lime. He decides to do this, just in case. When his mother sees the bag of lime in the garage and asks him about it, he tells her that with Dad gone he will take care of the yard. She smiles. "Good boy," she says.

While prepping the yard he finds pieces of concrete from a pond his father had tried to build. Last year Lenny saw his father digging a pit in the back yard. He had taken off his shirt and shoveled the earth with a fervor Lenny hadn't seen before. He stabbed the ground, his back muscles twisting, and threw the earth onto a growing pile. Lenny walked outside and watched. Without breaking his rhythm his father told Lenny that he was building a pond that would have fish and turtles. He would have water lilies and smooth stones. He would have a small fountain that would spout water.

He went back to work. After a while he grew tired and

asked Lenny to help him dig out the larger rocks. Lenny used a gardening spade to pry out fist-sized quartz, and was startled to find a large bone, which he thought might be from a dinosaur but which Ed would later tell him was a cow bone. Much of this area had been farmland.

Over the next week his father finished digging out the hole, which was about the size of a shallow grave, and one Saturday morning he mixed a few bags of concrete with soil and rocks, and began lining the pond. Something didn't seem right to Lenny, though, when he saw how the concrete caked at the bottom. Ed also saw this and looked at the concrete bags closely. He turned to Lenny, made a face, and shook his head. Later he told Lenny that their father had added soil to pre-mixed concrete, ruining it. But at the time Ed had just made a disgusted face and walked away.

When their father finished cementing the pond, he let it dry for a few days and then tested it by running a garden hose to it and turning the water on. Lenny watched from the back steps. The concrete was rocky and dirty, the hole misshapen, and as the murky water rose up bits of debris floated to the top. His father let the water reach ground level, and turned off the hose. He then used a broom to clean off the top. He looked down at the dirty brown water. He peered closer. The water was slowly receding. He turned the hose back on and refilled the pond. But after a few minutes the water level fell. Obviously the cement had leaks.

He pulled out the hose and stared at the receding dirty water. Lenny knew the pond was nothing like his father had envisioned, and to Lenny's young eyes he thought it looked more like a muddy trench. Lenny watched him coil up the hose and walk back into the house. Lenny moved closer to

the pond to inspect it, and could only see swirls of dirt beneath the clotted surface.

The empty pond sat there for a few weeks until his father
filled it in with dirt and never mentioned it again.

Lenny sees Sal again on his new motorcycle, but this time
he has a girl riding with him, hugging his waist. She wears
a helmet, but her long blond hair flutters from her neck. Sal
pulls up to Lenny and tells him that he's quitting the business. The girl takes off her helmet and flips her hair back.
She has wide, blue eyes and freckles on her nose.

"This is my girlfriend."

She gives Lenny a gorgeous smile, and he suddenly feels
shy.

Sal says, "I want to go to college. I got my high school
degree and am going to Nassau Community. I'm getting my
shit together."

"That's great," Lenny says.

"I have seeds if you want them. Let me know. I'm definitely not going to use them."

"Why don't you sell them?"

"I'm done buying and selling—"

"And using," his girlfriend adds.

"And using."

When can I get them?"

"No hurry. Those are sealed and good for a while. Come
by whenever."

His girlfriend puts the helmet back on, and Sal waves to
Lenny before riding away.

Lenny has never seen him with a girl before, and as they
disappear down the street he feels lonely. He walks up to

the train station, lays down some pennies and, while waiting for the train, he calls Nancy. But the number has been disconnected. He tries again and then calls the operator who says that the number hasn't been changed, but turned off.

He thanks her and hangs up. He remembers Nancy mentioning working at a camp during the summer. He sits down on a bench and wonders why he doesn't have more friends.

A train approaches, and he stands near the edge of the platform, looking down at his pennies. The train stops, a few commuters walk out, the conductors peering out of the windows, and the train pulls out of the station.

Lenny jumps down to collect his squashed and warped pennies. A woman yells, "Hey! What are you doing?"

He turns and sees an elderly woman with a Macy's shopping bag rushing toward him. She says, "Get back up here! You shouldn't be down there!"

He ignores her, pocketing the pennies, two of which are almost perfectly oval-sized. The woman glares down over the edge and says, "Young man, you can get killed down there."

"I'm fine." He hoists himself up onto the platform, and dusts off his jeans.

"How would you like me to tell your father what you're doing?"

He says, "My father is dead."

She blinks, startled. "Oh. I'm sorry."

"He died last month. Heart attack."

"Oh. I... I..."

"He died in front of me."

"I'm so sorry."

He walks away. The strange thing is that the story feels

true.

Lenny will see his father only a handful of times over
the next decade, and the final confrontation—which will in-
volve his father refusing to acknowledge any fault in the
violence in their house—allows Lenny to cut all ties with
him. His father, then, does die in Lenny's mind, for after the
break Lenny never sees him again.

34

The chores multiply. In addition to cooking, washing dishes, laundry and yard work, Lenny also has to vacuum the house. Mira is supposed to empty the garbage cans once a week, but she never does. He has to remind her dozens of times, and she just doesn't seem to care. He ends up doing her chores, because no matter how much he hounds her, the garbage cans overflow.

Mira becomes secretive, refusing to tell him where she goes. When Lenny tells her to come home for dinner, she says, "You're not my parent."

"I'm in charge when Mom's not here."

"No, you're not."

"You better listen to me."

"Or what? You're going to tell on me? I'll tell Mom that you have a lot money from somewhere."

He freezes. "What did you say?"

"I know about all the money you have."

"What are you talking about?"

She taunts, "Secrets of the Bermuda Triangle?"

He grabs her arm and shoves her against the wall. Lenny had hollowed out the book to hide his cash. He yells, "Are you snooping in my room?"

"Ow! You're hurting me!"

"Did you take any of my money?"

"Where did you get all that?" she demands. "Did you steal it?"

"You searched my room!"

"Let go!"

He lets go of her arm, but blocks her way from leaving the kitchen. He says, "You went through my things? You know that's wrong. How would you like it if I did that in your room?"

"I bet you stole it. I know you go sneaking out at night sometimes."

He steps back, not sure how to respond to this. "Did you tell Mom?"

"No, but I will if you're not nice to me."

He shakes his head. "When did you get so mean?"

Her face crumples. "I'm not mean."

"We have to be sticking together."

She looks down, about to cry. He punches her lightly on the shoulder and tells her it's okay. "But please don't go through my room anymore."

She nods her head, still looking down.

When he returns to his room, he takes the cash out of the Bermuda Triangle book, and tries to think of a new hiding spot. Nothing seems safe enough; he needs a new bank account, and will research this after lunch. He needs a nap. It's exhausting, acting like an adult.

Bringing home the paperwork for his mother to sign, since he can't have his own account until he's eighteen, Lenny waits for her to return from work. This Children's Savings Account at the local bank doesn't need parental permission for deposits or withdrawals, so it's ideal for his unmonitored saving and spending.

She comes home late, and studies the forms, amused.

She asks how much money he has saved, and he tells her he plans to close his joint account with Dad, which has thirty dollars in it.

"Why do you want to close that one?"

"My friend Sal said not to trust joint accounts. Dad can steal it."

She laughs. "He won't steal thirty dollars from you."

He tells her about the car dent repair bill, and how his father had lied, making Lenny work more than he should have. His mother sighs. "I didn't know that." She signs the paperwork, and fills out the rest of the information. She then reaches into her purse and pulls out a checkbook. "Let me help you with the account."

"That's okay."

"No, just a little." She writes a check for twenty dollars. As she tears it out, she says, "You should start saving for college. I don't know how we will pay for all that."

Lenny's dreams have been getting more and more vivid, and he suspects it's because he sleeps more deeply. With his father gone and their evenings quiet, he finds himself relaxing more quickly, and sinking into a sleep that often knocks him out until morning. It's almost as if he's catching up on years of deprivation. But his dreams are usually frightening, often puzzling, and when he wakes up he lies still for a while, remembering the fleeting details. His jaw aches. His head hurts. He replays the images in his head, disturbed by the repetition of the same kind of dream—being chased, hiding, running—and even though he knows that these are variations of the same memories, it doesn't make his mornings any easier.

This pattern of deep but disquieting sleep will continue throughout his life, with his teeth-grinding worsening over the years to the point of cracking his molars and wearing his incisors down to stumps. He will add hair-pulling and unconscious thrashing soon, but at this moment the vivid nightmares and jaw-clenching battles prefigure a significant shift, when violent days and sleepless nights become peaceful days but violent nights.

35

When their father would sit at the dinner table with them, drunk and expansive, he would often tell them how he had always wanted to be a doctor. Even after coming to the United States to study finance, he dreamed of switching over to biology and then applying to medical school. And every time he told the story he would add that having a baby, Ed, made it impossible. Usually Ed was there, and Mira and Lenny knew better than to look at him, but Lenny sensed Ed's exhaustion with the topic, with being blamed for thwarting their father's dreams. Ed sat stone-faced and unmoving, folding his arms and ignoring his food.

Their father often lied about where he had gone to school, claiming he had his PhD from Columbia, though in reality he had been a teaching assistant there for a semester, and the PhD he did receive when he was in his forties was an honorary degree from a small religious college that awarded it to him in appreciation for a donation.

At the dinner table, while he listened to his father ramble drunkenly about how close he had come to being a doctor, Lenny became good at feigning attention, staring and nodding his head but having almost no idea what his father was saying. His father's head would expand and contract in a psychedelic way, and Lenny would sometimes count rice grains on his plate to pass the time. Did you know a mound of white rice on a plate contains as many as a hundred mushy grains?

Lenny walks back to the house from somewhere—possibly
Radio Shack or the library—and notices his father's blue
Cadillac parked on the street around the corner. He stops
and stares, wondering if someone else had bought a similar
car, but then he sees the smoke rising from the driver's side,
and when he moves closer he sees his father sitting there,
flicking his ashes onto the street. What is he doing? Waiting? Spying? Meeting someone? Lenny stays hidden behind
a tree. After ten minutes Lenny concludes that his father is
spying.

His father blows his smoke straight ahead in the car, and
it swirls around him and slowly rises up out of the window. Lenny knows that his father misses them, but he won't
come to the house because Lenny's mother would probably call the police at this point. She grows stronger every
day she spends without him. Lenny watches his father for
another few minutes. He then backtracks and wanders the
neighborhood.

Later that evening, when his mother finally returns home
from work, Lenny tells her about the spying, and she says,
"Yes, I've seen him. I think he also calls and hangs up. He
misses his children."

Lenny says, "We don't miss him."

His mother turns to him, surprised. She studies him for a
moment, and says, "He's still your father."

"A bad one."

She sighs. "Sometimes you can be as hard as him."

This startles Lenny, who says, "That's not true."

She smiles, and shrugs it off.

Lenny finds Mira in the living room watching TV and drawing on looseleaf paper. Her art teacher told her at the end of the school year that she has a gift for drawing, and this is all the encouragement she needs to dive into it during the summer. He asks her if she wants to explore the church, but she doesn't.

He says, "You can find stuff to draw in there."

She looks outside and replies, "It's too dark."

They haven't been spending any time together, and although he likes not having her tag along, he's lonely. He asks, "You want to see what's playing at Gables?" The movie theater recently began a 99-cent promotion.

"No, I just want to watch TV and draw."

He's about to tease her, grab her paper and taunt her with it, but he remembers his mother's comment, that he can be as hard as his father. This rankles him, so he goes downstairs and watches his illegal cable TV and reads about strategies of guerrilla outdoor marijuana farming.

Many years later both his sister and brother will echo his mother's sentiments, that Lenny, according to Ed, is "scarily like Dad." Ed will point out Lenny's military style—waking at dawn, maintaining a strict, rigorous schedule, even an instinctive, methodical, warrior-like way of getting what he wants—that can't help but remind them of their father. This will hurt Lenny more than he will admit, since he will strive his entire life not to be like his father. He will argue that he is what his father could not become—disciplined and focused. But Mira will point out how Lenny can coldly, even cruelly, cut people out of his life, like he does with their father.

Lenny doesn't see this as cruel, but justified—that the people he cuts out of his life are dangerous to him, and need excising. In this way he is the opposite of his mother, who gave their father too many years of second chances.

36

But it's true that Lenny does have a very disciplined approach to everything during this time; he trains almost every day, practicing both tae kwon do and kung fu, and teaches himself all kinds of useful and, for the most part, illegal skills, everything from building a microwave antenna from coffee cans that receives a new premium TV service, to finding hacked long-distance card numbers, to using a whistle from a Captain Crunch cereal box that coincidentally has the same tone to trick a payphone into giving him free calls. All this information is readily available to anyone who digs, and Lenny likes to dig.

He buys an inexpensive Atari computer—the keyboard isn't even real but has a flat membrane that's so hard to press he can only use his index finger reinforced with his middle finger to type. He buys a cheap dial-up modem and joins bulletin boards—the earliest incarnation of forums—where he learns even more from the hacking community.

He worries about his father spying on them, so learns more about surveillance, but by the time he builds a telescoping periscope that allows him to see the street from his basement, his father stops showing up. His mother says the hang-ups also stopped. She guesses that he probably found another woman.

Lenny also continues his casual but persistent interest in marijuana cultivation. This is the most compelling of his investigations, his self-education, because he has already earned more money by helping Sal than he has in his entire young life. Without having any real concrete plans, he begins preparing the back yard for a possible crop, tilling the various plots near the foundation and in his mother's old garden. He fertilizes the soil to prepare for the sowing after the first frost.

He has no seeds yet, but reads in a new magazine called *High Times* about a store in New York that buys seeds in Canada for "ornamental purposes" and resells them in the city. He looks up the store, which is listed as a natural food grocery, and he plots a future trip into Manhattan.

It surprises him how easy all of this is—he only needs time and money and energy, all three of which he has in plenty, given that it's summer vacation and he has a wad of cash from Sal. He also spends more time reading novels at the air-conditioned library. He discovers the young adult science fiction section, and devours stories about spaceships, time travel and aliens, and is so moved by one time-travel novel in which the protagonist went to Ancient Egypt that he writes a letter to the author.

The librarian explains to him how to write authors in care of the publishers, and he likes the idea of being able to contact anyone through the mail. He writes Jimmy Carter, asking about space travel, and receives an embossed thank you card and a signed photo of the Carter family. He writes TV and movie stars, including Mark Hamill from *Star Wars*, the cast of *Eight is Enough* and *Three's Company*, and authors like Robert Heinlein and Isaac Asimov. He even writes the cast of *Brady Bunch*, but the letters come back Return to Sender, because he didn't realize he was watching all the shows in reruns.

The letters to celebrities and authors, many of whom either send back photos or short notes, make him feel connected to the world beyond his little neighborhood, and when he learns about a pen pal program run through the library, where he will be given an address of a student his age from somewhere in Asia, he signs up.

He's lonely, isolated, and spends most of his time by himself, but begins using reading and writing as a way to keep connected. He misses the time with Sal and on a couple of occasions goes looking for him at his house, but his sister says he's with his girlfriend.

Lenny wonders how he can get a girlfriend.

Ed calls home and speaks to their mother briefly, telling her how much he loves California. He weighs the notion of canceling his plans to go to SUNY Binghamton and reapplying to schools around Los Angeles, but because he's a New York resident Binghamton would be cheaper. He'll have to take a year off from school to establish California residency, which their mother doesn't want him to do. He speaks briefly to Lenny, telling him that he'd love it out there, since the weather is great and the beaches are the best he has ever seen.

This is the seed that plants itself in Lenny's mind, and California will be his destination years later, where he will live near the beach, and where he will find the memories of this time resurfacing during his fortieth year, and feel compelled to write this book.

One evening Lenny's mother comes home and tells him about police cars and fire engines converging a couple blocks away, near the library. The streets have been cordoned off because of a big accident. Lenny wants to go out and check, but she brought home dinner, McDonald's, and he's torn between eating his Big Mac and seeing the police action. In the end the French fries win out.

The next morning he walks over to the scene, to Narwood Avenue, but sees no evidence of the activity. He goes into the library and asks the librarian about the police cars here yesterday. She says, "It was a motorcycle accident. Some poor guy crashed his motorcycle into a car."

The mention of a motorcycle makes him straighten up. He asks if she knows the name of the motorcyclist.

"No. I heard he wasn't wearing a helmet. I heard he died."

"How would I find out who it was?"

"The local newspaper will have it in the next edition."

"Can I find out sooner?"

"Why?"

"It might've been a friend of mine."

The librarian pauses, and says, "I'm sorry. Yes, you can call the local police. But you can also call your friend's parents to check."

Lenny walks the few blocks to Sal's house. As soon as he sees the flowers on the doorstep, he knows. He approaches the front door slowly, already dreading the news, and rings the bell. Sal's sister appears, and she has a blank, muted expression on her face. Lenny asks her if Sal is home.

She shakes her head. "He was killed yesterday."

"Oh."

"He crashed his motorcycle."

"Oh."

They stand there for a minute, and then she closes the door.

37

Lenny walks around the neighborhood slowly, not quite be-lieving any of this, and finds himself heading to the swamp. A few kids he hasn't seen before play on the rope that ex-tends over the creek, though none of them jump in. They swing over the water and back, and then stumble onto the bank. He watches them for a while, smiling when one of them accidentally falls into the water and leaps out, disgust-ed.

Lenny takes the convoluted paths to the grow site, where he finds the cut stalks depressing. A few leaves lie dried and withered in the scuffed dirt. The tripwires are still here, even though Sal had trampled them into the ground.

Then Lenny remembers the seeds in Sal's crawlspace. It won't take long for his parents to find those, and when that happens, they will be upset.

He hurries out of the woods and to Sal's house again. The crawlspace door is on the side of the house, accessible simply by cutting through their side yard, and is covered with thick bushes and a row of young saplings. When he sneaks along the side of the house, he stays well below the windows. He can hear a TV blaring from one of the rooms. The crawlspace door is locked, but Lenny still has the extra on his keychain.

He unlocks the door and climbs in. He notices immedi-ately that Sal had already cleared out most of his drug-relat-ed materials, including the shelf of books and pamphlets. He used to have a bong and a small box of rolling papers here, both of which are missing. Lenny smells air freshener—lavender—that mingles with the faint hints of pot. He crawls to the corner, where a large plastic storage bin sits among a few scattered mini-bike parts and a radio. When he pries open the top, he finds the jar of seeds—little brown pellets filled to the top with a few dried leaves and tiny stems mashed in. He doesn't see any other evidence of drugs, and suspects this had been part of Sal's new outlook.

He hears footsteps upstairs. He knows he can't be caught here, so he quickly carries out the heavy jar, relocking the door quietly. Sal's mother is directly upstairs, talking into a phone. Her voice sounds depleted and exhausted. Lenny waits until she drifts into a different part of the house and then he hurries out of the yard and down the street, cradling the jar in his arms.

He feels guilty for stealing something from a dead friend, but justifies it as keeping Sal's parents from discovering anything.

When he returns home he hurries downstairs and searches for a hiding place. There are no locks to the basement and he worries about his sister snooping again, so he decides the best thing to do is not to hide it. Marijuana seeds resemble some varieties of maple seeds, so he tapes on a label "maple seeds for replanting tree" and leaves this on his shelf.

But his next project is to build a safe.

Late that night he finds his mother at her home office, the desk lamp the only light on in the house, so the glow fills the hallway. She looks up, and asks why he's awake. He tells her he's having trouble sleeping, and she motions for him to sit in the chair across from her. When he does, he mentions that the motorcycle accident had been with Sal.

"That older boy?" she asks, alarmed.

"He died."

"Oh, no." She closes her eyes for a moment. "His mother... I met her a few times. She must be... Oh, this is terrible."

"It was a new motorcycle. He wanted that for a long time."

"Are you okay? Are you sad?"

"I don't know. I guess not. I didn't see him that much anymore."

"But still. He was your friend."

They sit quietly. She asks if he's getting ready for school, which starts in a couple weeks.

"I guess so," he says, then asks how he is supposed to do well.

She smiles. "Do everything your teacher tells you."

"That's all?"

"Study very hard for all the tests."

This isn't very satisfying advice, so he resolves to go to the library to learn more about how to do well in school.

"Do you miss your father?"

"No," he replies, surprised by the question.

"Your father canceled our insurance without telling me. I found out by accident. We weren't covered with health insurance and car insurance for a few weeks. It was really bad of him."

"Do you have insurance now?"

"We all do. Yes. It's not the canceling—there's no reason why he should pay my car insurance. It's not telling me that's…. He can be so…" She stops herself. She takes a deep breath and asks if he wants something to eat or drink.

"No. I'll go back to bed."

"Give me a kiss goodnight."

He kisses her cheek and she touches his arm. "Are you sure you're okay? About Sal?"

"I think so."

"I can't imagine what Sal's mother is going through. If there's a funeral service, do you want to go?"

He wonders if Tommy and Sal's other friends would be there. He replies, "No."

"Okay. Go to bed."

Lenny stays up late and watches a horror movie on cable TV, a creepy story about little creatures that come out only in the dark. By the time the movie is over, it's almost two in the morning, and he can't bring himself to turn off the lights. He studies the marijuana pamphlets, the jar of seeds in his line of vision, and he wonders about cultivating a small crop. He has no idea what he would do with the harvest, but he has all these seeds. It seems like a waste not to try them.

While leafing through a catalog that lists books about lockpicking and safecracking, he wonders if Sal would appreciate a book on lockpicking. Then he remembers that Sal is dead. Slowly it dawns on him that anyone, even he, can die randomly and suddenly. He has trouble grappling with the implications. He makes a mental note to look up more information about this at the library. It seems he can find all the answers there.

38

Lenny feels the full repercussions later, when he sees Sal's sister walking home one afternoon. She is always quiet, and whenever he sees her around the neighborhood she nods to him, but they never talk. One afternoon, just a week or so before the first day of school, Lenny wanders home from Radio Shack and sees Terry by herself, staring down at the sidewalk as she turns the corner. She's avoiding the cracks, Lenny can tell, from the way she steps awkwardly forward, almost jumping ahead.

He follows her, though he doesn't know why. She isn't heading back to her house, and Lenny is curious.

Compared to her late brother, Terry is short and muscular—she plays softball and volleyball—and doesn't look very much like Sal except for a longish face. She walks toward Robinhood's, a sporting goods store on Sunrise Highway, but doesn't enter. Instead, she stares through the display windows, her hands shoved into her pockets, her shoulders hunched.

She continues window shopping. Lenny thinks about Mira, and how she would feel if he died, and then knows how lonely he'd be if something happened to his sister.

Terry just stands there. She stares into the window for a long time, and then Lenny sees that she isn't focusing on anything in particular. Her gaze is unfocused and distant. He can't bear to watch her any longer. He slips away and returns home.

The countdown to the new school year preoccupies Lenny, and he draws big red x's on his calendar as the first day approaches. He knows he'll lose his free time, and steps up his martial arts training and library research, including learning more about marijuana cultivation. He also begins taking trips into Manhattan, finding the bookstores and newsstands that carry esoteric magazines. It's so easy to get into the city, the train heading directly into Penn Station, and then all he has to do is walk up the steps from the station and there are half a dozen magazine stores within a block.

Years later, when he will look back on this pivotal period in his life he sees that it helped define him: he became independent, and he discovered a sense of his self that could only emerge from solitude. His desire to become a writer wouldn't take hold for another few years, but the discipline required of that job had its origins during this time, when he understood that the key to finishing anything isn't the initial enthusiastic rush but the slow and steady daily effort.

He is also getting physically stronger and more flexible. By the end of the summer he can do full splits and graceful kicks over his head. He has no idea if his form is textbook, but he emulates with ease the kicks and hand strikes he sees on the kung-fu movies. Soon he'll buy a VCR after researching the differences between VHS and Betamax, and he will teach himself tae kwon do from instructional videos. That, and taking lessons from a local studio, will eventually get him good enough so that he'll join his college tae kwon do team, and he'll even perform on stage in Seoul.

But it starts with punching and kicking a tree in his back

yard and listening to kung-fu movies as he falls asleep.

One afternoon he wants to see the sunset from the bell tower. The ideal location would've been the train station, but he doesn't want to deal with the late afternoon commuters who crowd the platform during rush hour. So he jimmies the back door of the church and climbs up to the tower. He sits on the west-facing banister, and looks out over the neighborhood. From this vantage point he can see the library and Narwood Avenue, where Sal died. The sun is setting.

He read in a kung-fu book how Shaolin monks would meditate at sunrise and sunset, and although he has tried meditating at sunrise, he has trouble focusing, his mind spinning with everything he has to do. Reading and exercising seem to be better for him in the morning. But now, in the early evenings as he begins to wind down, it's easier for him to calm his thoughts.

Lenny sits cross-legged and practices his breathing. He watches the sun fall slowly behind the trees as the sky turns orange. He empties his mind and tries to focus on steadying his breath. As he inhales and exhales, the sun drops below the horizon and the sky turns purple, and he feels a momentary and immense welling of emotion, of happiness and serenity and centeredness that startles him. Then the feeling disappears. He slows his breathing even further, trying to recapture the feeling, but he can't. It will be almost twenty-five years until he can find again that one moment of peace, when he will be rock climbing in the Sierras, and one morning he will scale a huge boulder at sunrise, sharing the top with a lizard, watching the sun warm the mountains.

Lenny remembers a time when the family was together, shortly after their move to Long Island when their father still had a good job. Because of the tumult of settling into a new house and new neighborhood they were all bound by the unfamiliarity of their surroundings. One night they went to a local restaurant, Beefsteak Charlie's, which his father wanted to try because of their All You Can Eat shrimp.

They sat in a large booth, the lights dim and the noises muted by thick curtains hanging along the walls. After they filled their plates with shrimp and salad from the buffet bar, their father told them a story about when he first came to the United States. He had been through the Korean War, with all kinds of food shortages, especially beef, so when he started graduate school in Florida and saw steak and seafood houses everywhere, he couldn't believe it.

"I ate steak every night for a week until I got sick," he told them. He pointed to the menu in front of him. "Look at all the different kinds of steak! This is America, the land of steak."

Their mother laughed and said something to him in Korean. He smiled. Ed announced that he wanted a big rare steak, and Mira said she wanted ice cream.

"Steak and ice cream together?" their father said.

Mira made a face, making him laugh. Lenny wouldn't know this until later, but this was one of the only times they ever had a normal, fun family dinner.

He has searched his memory for more good family times like these, but none surface. No, the good memories occur later when, as adults, he and his siblings reconnect with each other and their mother, when he talks to them about this time, although, curiously, he seems to recall small, eso-teric details that no one else does.

Lenny, as a child, has glimmers of understanding that every moment, good or bad, joyful or frightening, means something. Perhaps this is, ultimately, what draws him to become a writer, for it's the details and their significance that stay with him without his even trying.

He knows, for example, even as a kid, that the last time he and Mira break into the church, at the end of that sum-mer, is important, somehow. He suspects this because, first, it's morning. Mira wants to play her viola on stage, but when they enter the main sanctuary area and stand on the pulpit, they're surprised by the bright sun shining through the stained glass windows. They had always come here in the late afternoon or evening, so the eastern-facing win-dows have never been illuminated. But now, this morning, the pews are brilliant with greens and blues, and the shafts of dusty sunlight beam down onto the worn red carpeting.

Mira and Lenny stand there for a moment, awed, reg-istering the beauty. Mira then pulls out her viola, tunes it, and begins playing scales. She sits on the dais leading up to the pulpit, and warms up her fingers. Lenny sits in the front pew and listens while staring up at the stained glass images of circles and suns and glowing crosses highlighted with rays of light. Mira then plays what Lenny later learns is a simplified version of a Bach sonata, and although she's tentative at first, the notes squeaky, she soon repeats it with more confidence, and Lenny sits back, feeling that this mo-ment is special. He knows that the end of this summer marks the end of a tumultuous time in their family. He knows that a new school, new friends, the beginning of a new life, await all of them. And when he watches his sister playing a sonata in the brilliant sunlight, her face beaming with delight, and he stares up at the stained glass windows colorful and radiant, he knows he has to remember this moment, remember this image, because it makes him truly and deeply happy.

ACKNOWLEDGMENTS

Thanks to my first readers: Frances Sackett, Linda Davis, Claudette Groenendaal and Jillian Lauren; to my editor of eighteen years, Jerry Gold; to the Merrick Library; to the many Los Angeles friends who helped me get situated, including the Chehaks, the Erspamers, and Carole Kirschner; to my friends at *Awake* and *Justified*; to my mother Umee Chang Pepe, my brother Ed Chang, my sister-in-law Raafia Mazhar Chang, my sister Mira Chang; and a special thanks to Toni Ann Johnson for everything.

Many names have been changed to protect the innocent and not-so-innocent. Although my mother and siblings checked and verified this account with their recollections, any errors and misremembrances are entirely mine.